HOLIDAY WITH THE BEST MAN

BY

KATE HARDY

First published in Great Britain 2016
By Mills & Boon, an imprint of HarperCollins*Publishers*
1 London Bridge Street, London, SE1 9GF

Large Print edition 2016

© 2016 Pamela Brooks

ISBN: 978-0-263-26226-1

Printed and bound in Great Britain
by CPI Antony Rowe, Chippenham, Wiltshire

HOLIDAY WITH
THE BEST MAN

To Gay, the best stepmum in the world.

PROLOGUE

ROLAND'S FACE ACTUALLY ached from smiling, but he knew he had to keep it up. Apart from the fact that it was his best friend's wedding day—and of course Roland was delighted that Hugh had found the love of his life—he also knew that half the guests were remembering that Roland's wife had been killed in a car accident nearly two years ago, and were worrying that he was finding it hard to cope with today.

As he'd said to Hugh at the altar, today had brought back good memories of his own wedding day. Roland just hoped that Hugh and Bella would have a lot more years of happiness together than he and Lynette had had—and none of the misery that they'd both kept secret, even from their family and their closest friends.

He knew he ought to make the effort to go and

dance with the chief bridesmaid. Even though his friend Hugh had opted to have two best men, and Tarquin—the other best man—was dancing with Bella's sister right now, Roland knew that he couldn't use that as an excuse. If he didn't dance with Grace, everyone would assume that it was because he was thinking of Lynette, and the last thing he wanted right now was another dose of pity. He'd had more than enough of that after the crash.

One dance. He could do that. All he had to do was ignore the fact that the ballroom in the Elizabethan manor house was full of fairy lights, creating the most romantic mood. And to ignore his misgivings about the chief bridesmaid, because it wasn't his place to judge her—even though the little he knew about her pressed all the wrong buttons. Grace had been so drunk the first time she'd met Hugh, that she'd thrown up over him in the taxi; plus she'd cancelled her wedding at the last minute. Sure, everyone had an off day or made mistakes, but to Roland it sounded as if Grace was a spoiled princess who liked alcohol too much.

And a spoiled, princessy drunk driver had shattered Roland's life with her selfishness, nearly two years ago. Having to be nice to a woman like that for even a few minutes really stuck in his craw. But he'd do it for his best friend's sake. His best friend who, even now, was dancing with his bride—and Roland was pretty sure that the glow around Hugh and Bella was due to more than just the fairy lights. This was real happiness.

Which left him to man up and do his duty. Right now Grace looked perfectly demure in her dark red bridesmaid's dress with its ballerina skirt and sweetheart neckline, and she was even wearing flat shoes rather than spindly heels so she didn't tower over the bride. Though her dark hair was in a sophisticated up-do with wisps of hair curled into ringlets that framed her face—a seriously high-maintenance style—and her eyelashes had most definitely been enhanced. So maybe Roland was right about the princessy tendencies. And even Tarquin—who saw the good in everyone—had admitted that Grace was nothing like sweet, bubbly little Bella.

One dance, he reminded himself. Do your duty and don't let your best friend down.

At the end of the song, he walked over to Grace and Tarquin. 'As the other best man, I believe the next dance is meant to be mine,' he said, forcing himself to keep smiling.

'It is indeed,' Tarquin said, and clapped him on the shoulder. 'See you later, Grace.'

'See you later, Tarquin,' she echoed, then turned to Roland. 'I don't think we've been properly introduced yet. I'm Bella's sister, Grace. You're Roland, aren't you?'

'Yes.'

'Nice to meet you.' She held out her hand to shake his.

Thinking, oh, please, just hurry up and let us get this over with, Roland took her hand and shook it. And he was truly shocked to find a prickle of awareness running down his spine.

Close up, Grace Faraday had the most incredible eyes: a deep cornflower blue. Her mouth was a perfect cupid's bow. Her complexion was fresh, almost dewy. And there was something that drew him to her. Something that made him feel protective.

And that really threw him.

Based on what he'd heard from the two people whose opinion he trusted most in the world, Roland had expected to dislike the woman. Instead, he found himself attracted to her. Attracted to someone he'd been sure was the last woman he'd ever want to date. And he really didn't know what to do about it.

'It was a lovely wedding, wasn't it?' Grace said. 'And that song Hugh wrote for Bella—that was amazing.'

'Mmm,' Roland said, too confused to string a coherent sentence together, and gave her his best attempt at a smile.

Grace was shocked by how different Hugh's two best friends were. Tarquin had been sweet and funny, and she'd felt really comfortable with him; Roland was taciturn to the point of making Grace feel awkward and shy, the way she usually was with strangers.

It didn't help that she'd felt a weird prickle of

awareness when he'd shaken her hand. By any standards, Roland was good-looking, and the tail-coat, dark trousers, dark red waistcoat and matching cravat he wore emphasised it even more. His dark hair was brushed back from his forehead, and his slightly olive skin was clean-shaven. He could've been a model for a wedding suit company, and Grace wasn't sure if she found that more attractive or intimidating.

Maybe if she treated this as work—if she was professional and sensible with him, the way she'd be with a client—they could get through this dance without it being a total disaster.

Not having a clue what to say to him, she went through the motions of dancing with him and really hoped that pinning a smile to her face would be enough to get her through the next song. Just as well she'd talked Bella into letting her wear flat shoes; if she'd worn heels, she would probably have tripped over Roland's feet and made a complete and utter fool of herself.

Though it felt odd to be dancing with someone who was six inches taller than she was. Howard, her ex-fiancé, had been five foot eight, so she'd always worn flat shoes to make him feel less self-conscious about the fact that she was the same height as he was. Roland was broad-shouldered, where Howard had been slight. Being in his arms made Grace feel petite and feminine—something she wasn't used to. She was sensible, no-nonsense, and way too tall to be treated as if she was fragile.

She noticed that Roland's dark eyes were watchful. Why did he look so wary? Grace wondered.

Then she realised with a sinking heart just why she was feeling so awkward with him: because Roland was looking at her in exactly the same way that Howard's mother always had. Rather than smiling back at her, his lips were thinned. It was pretty clear that he'd judged her and decided that she wasn't quite good enough.

No wonder he wasn't chatting to her, the way Tarquin had. The guy clearly disliked her—even though he'd never met her before.

Well, that was his problem. She'd be polite and dance with him to this song, fulfilling their duty as the chief bridesmaid and the best man. Then she'd make sure she stayed out of his way for the rest of the evening, spending her time with her parents and Hugh's family.

And as for that weird prickle of awareness just now—well, that was just how weddings made everyone feel. Especially a glitzy wedding like this one, held in the grounds and ballroom of a manor house that had been in Hugh's family for generations. Yet behind the glamour was a warm-hearted, loving family who adored Grace's bubbly, slightly unconventional baby sister for who she was. And Grace had seen Roland hugging Bella earlier—with a proper smile on his face—so clearly he liked Grace's sister.

But this taciturn, slightly forbidding man clearly wasn't going to extend that warmth to Grace. And she absolutely refused to let it get to her. Why should his opinion of her matter? She didn't know anything about him, other than that he was Hugh's other best friend from school and was a sleeping partner in Hugh's record label. But, even if Roland was single, he was the last man Grace would even consider dating. She wasn't going to repeat her mistake with How-ard. The next man she dated would be one who made her heart skip a beat and who'd sweep her off her feet. Someone who'd make her feel good about herself.

Which meant absolutely not Roland whatever-his-name-was.

Even if he was one of the most good-looking men she'd ever met.

CHAPTER ONE

Two days later

YET AGAIN GRACE missed Bella. Her little sister
was the person she most wanted to call and talk
to about her job interview today. But Bella was
in San Francisco right now with Hugh and, even
without having to take into account the eight-
hour time difference, Grace had no intention of
interrupting her baby sister's honeymoon. She'd
wait for Bella's daily 'postcard' text, and casually mention in her reply that she thought the interview had gone OK. And hopefully later in the
week she'd be able to report good news.

Please let her have got the job.

Temping was fine, but Grace knew that she
functioned at her best with a solid structure in
her life, and when she was able to plan more than
just a couple of days ahead. The last couple of

months, since she'd called off her own wedding, had changed her entire life. Not only had her relationship ended, she'd lost her job and her home because of it, too.

Bella was the bubbly one who coped just fine with change and seizing the day, always living life to the full; whereas Grace was more cautious, weighing things up and doing the sensible thing every single time. Even though calling off the wedding had been the right thing to do, it had caused her a huge amount of heartache and guilt. Bella had stood by her, as had their parents. But Grace hated the ensuing chaos.

At least she had a flat of her own again now. She'd been let down at the last minute with the flat she'd managed to find, but Bella as usual had been a bit scatty and forgotten to give her landlord her notice on time. And it had all worked out perfectly for both of them, because the landlord had agreed to let Grace take over the lease; she was just awaiting the paperwork. So that was another little bit of her life rebuilt.

Trying to push away the thought that she wasn't adjusting terribly well to her new life so far,

Grace opened the front door of the house that had been converted into three flats—and saw with horror that the hallway was an inch deep in water. *Water that was coming from underneath her front door.*

OK. Forget the panic and work with your common sense, the way you always do, she told herself. Turn off the water supply at the mains to stop any more water gushing out from wherever the leak is, turn off the electricity to avoid any problems there, run the taps to make sure the system drains fully, and *then* find out where the leak is coming from and call the landlord to organise a plumber.

Fortified now she had a plan to work to, Grace opened the flat's front door to find water everywhere. The carpet was soaked through and she could see from the change in the colour of the material that the water was soaking its way up into the sofa, too. What a *mess*. She took a deep breath, took off her shoes, and put them on the kitchen table along with her handbag and briefcase so they'd be out of the way of the water.

Stopcock. Where would the stopcock be? The

house had been converted into flats, so there was only a fifty-fifty chance that the stopcock would be inside her flat. But, to her relief, when she opened the cupboard under the sink in the hope that it was the most likely place to find the stopcock, the little wheel on the water pipe was clearly visible. She turned it off. Another switch dealt with the electricity supply, and when she went into the bathroom to turn on the taps to drain the system she could see the problem immediately: water was gushing through a burst pipe underneath the sink.

She grabbed the washing up bowl from the kitchen sink and put it there to catch the water that was still gushing from the burst pipe, then turned on the taps in the bath so the system would start to drain.

Those were the most important things. Now to call the landlord—and she really hoped that he'd be able to send an emergency plumber out to fix the pipe tonight. Though, even when the pipe was fixed and the water supply was back on, Grace knew that she was still going to have to find somewhere else to sleep tonight, because the flat was too badly flooded to be habitable. She'd also have to find somewhere to store all her stuff.

Although part of her wanted to burst into tears of sheer frustration and anger and misery, she knew that crying wasn't going to solve anything. She needed to stick with the practical stuff. Once she'd sorted that out, she could start weeping. But absolutely not until then.

There was a note in Bella's handwriting underneath a magnet on the door of the fridge, with a telephone number and the words, *Call if any problems.* Obviously this was the landlord's number; Grace was truly grateful that for once her little sister had been organised, despite spending the last three weeks knee-deep in plans for her whirlwind wedding to Hugh. Grace grabbed her mobile phone from her bag and called the number on the note.

Roland didn't recognise the number on his phone's screen, so he let the call go through to voicemail. A cold caller would give up as soon as Roland's recorded message started playing, and anyone who really wanted to talk to him could leave a message and he'd return the call when he had time.

There was an audible sigh on the answering machine. 'Hello. This is Grace Faraday.'

Bella's sister? Roland frowned. Why on earth would she be calling him?

'Please call me back urgently.' She said her telephone number slowly and clearly. 'If I haven't heard from you within thirty minutes, I'll call an emergency plumber and assume that you'll pick up the bill.'

Why did she need an emergency plumber? And why on earth did she think that *he'd* pay for the cost?

Intending to suggest that she called her landlord or her insurance company instead, he picked up the phone. 'Roland Devereux speaking.'

There was a stunned silence for a moment. 'Roland? As in Hugh's other best man Roland?' she asked.

'Yes.'

'Um, right—if you didn't catch the message I was in the middle of leaving, it's Bella's sister

Grace. There's a flood at the flat and I need an emergency plumber.' Her voice took on a slightly haughty tone. 'I assume that you, as the landlord, have a list of tradesmen you use.'

So *that* was why she thought he'd pay the bill for an emergency plumber. 'I'm not the landlord.'

'Ah. Sorry.' The haughtiness disappeared, and there was the slightest wobble in her voice. 'I don't suppose you know the landlord's contact details?'

Why on earth would he know something like that? 'No.'

'OK. Never mind.'

And there it was.

The tiniest sob. Muffled quickly, but he heard it.

It brought back all the memories of Lynette. Her heart-wrenching sobs every single month they'd failed to make a baby. The guilt about how badly he'd let her down and how he'd failed her at the last.

Plus Grace was his best friend's sister-in-law. If Roland's sister had called Hugh for help, Hugh would've come straight to Philly's rescue. So Roland knew he had to do the right thing.

'I'm sorry to have bother—' she began.

'Grace. How bad is the flood?' he cut in.

'You've just told me you're not the landlord, so don't worry about it.'

He winced, but he knew that he deserved the slightly acidic tone in her voice. But there was one thing that was bothering him. 'Where did you get my number?'

'Bella left me a note on the fridge—a phone number for emergencies.' She sighed. 'Again, I apologise. I assumed it was the landlord's number. Obviously I was wrong.'

That didn't matter right now. He was focused on the flood. 'Have you turned off the water?'

'Yes. I'm not an airhead,' she said drily. 'I also turned off the electricity supply to prevent any problems there, and I'm currently draining the system to try and stop any more water coming through. I need a plumber to fix the burst pipe, and I also need to tell the people in the flats upstairs, in case the problem in my flat has affected their water supply, too.'

He was surprised that Grace sounded so capable and so organised. It didn't fit with what he'd been told about her. But she'd said there was a burst pipe, and clearly she didn't have a number to call for help—apart from his, which Bella had left her in case of emergencies. He could hardly just hang up and leave her to it. 'What's the address?' he asked abruptly.

'Why?'

'Because you just called me for help,' he said.

'Mistakenly,' she said crisply. 'For which I apologise. Yet again.'

'Bella obviously left you my number in case of emergencies—and a burst pipe counts as an emergency.' Although Bella had forgotten to tell him she'd given Grace his number, that wasn't Grace's fault. 'Where are you?'

'Bella's flat.'

'I don't actually know the address,' Roland explained.

'Oh. Right.' Sounding slightly reluctant, she told him the address.

'OK. I'm on my way.'

'Are you a plumber or something?'

'No, but I know a good one. I'll call him on the way and have him on standby in case you can't get hold of the landlord.'

'Thank you,' Grace said. 'I appreciate this.'

Roland called his plumber from the car, warning him that it was possibly a storm in a teacup but asking him to stay on standby. But, when he turned up at the flat, he discovered that Grace had been underplaying the situation, if anything. The water had clearly been gushing for a while and the carpets were soaked through; they'd need to be taken up and probably replaced. The sofa also needed to be moved, because water was seeping into it. And he felt another twinge of guilt as he noticed that Grace looked as if she'd been crying. Although she was clearly trying to be brave, this had obviously upset her.

'Did you manage to get in touch with the landlord?' he asked.

She shook her head. 'His details are probably somewhere in Bella's shoebox—but I'm not blaming her, because I should've checked everything properly myself before she and Hugh left. I live here now, so it's my responsibility.'

'Shoebox?' he asked, mystified.

'Bella's not really one for filing,' Grace explained. 'She has a shoebox system. Business receipts go in one shoebox, household stuff in another, and you just rummage through the shoeboxes when you want something.'

'That sounds a bit chaotic.' And it was definitely not the way Roland would do things. It wasted way too much time.

Grace shrugged. 'At least she has the shoeboxes now. It took a bit of nagging to get her that far.'

What? This didn't fit, at all. Wasn't Grace the drunken, princessy one? And yet right now she was wearing a sober grey suit and white shirt; plus that looked like a proper briefcase on the kitchen table, along with a pair of sensible black shoes and an equally sensible-looking handbag. Her nails weren't professionally manicured, her dark hair was cut simply in a long bob rather than being in a fussy high-maintenance style like the one she'd had at the wedding, and her make-up was minimal.

Maybe he'd got her totally wrong. More guilt flooded through him.

'The neighbours aren't home yet, so I've left a note on their doors to tell them what's happened,' she said. 'And I really need to find the landlord's details and check the insurance.'

Again, there was that tiny wobble in her voice.

'Are you OK?' he asked, hoping that she wasn't going to start crying.

'I've had better days.' She lifted her chin. 'And worse, for that matter. I'll live. Sorry. I would offer you a cup of tea but, as I don't have water or electricity right now...' She shrugged. 'I'm afraid I can't.'

'It's not a problem,' Roland said. 'My plumber's on standby, so I'll call him again to get him up to speed with the situation—and we need to shift that sofa in a minute before it soaks up any more water, to try and minimise the damage.'

'And the bookcase. And the bed. And...' She blew out a breath. 'It's just as well my car's a hatchback. I'm going to have to move everything I can out of here until this place dries out. And find somewhere for storage—though, as all my friends have flats just as tiny as this and none of them have a garage I can borrow, even temporarily. It's probably going to have to be one of those lock-up storage places.'

'Give me a moment.' Roland went outside and made a swift call to his plumber and then to one of the restoration specialist firms he'd used in the past. He also remembered seeing a café on the corner as he'd driven here; he made an executive decision to grab two takeaway black coffees, packets of sugar and two chocolate brownies. It would give them both enough energy to get through to the next stage. And if she didn't drink coffee—well, now would be a good time to start.

Grace had talked about finding a lock-up place to store the stuff from the flat. At this time of the evening, she'd be lucky to find somewhere to sort it out. And he had more than enough space to store her stuff. Even though part of him didn't really want to get involved, part of him knew that if something like this had happened to his sister, he'd want someone looking out for her. Grace was his best friend's sister-in-law. So that kind of made him responsible, didn't it?

On the way back to her flat, he called one of his team and asked him to bring a van.

She was already loading things into the back of her car when he got there.

'Coffee,' he said, and handed her one of the paper cups. 'I didn't know if you took milk or sugar, so I got it black and there are packets of sugar.'

'Thank you. How much do I owe you?' she asked.

He shook his head. 'It's fine. And I have a van on the way. Do you have some bags, boxes or suitcases I can start filling?'

'A van?' she asked, looking puzzled.

'The flat's small, but we're not going to be able to fit its entire contents into your car and mine,' he pointed out.

'So you hired a van?' Her eyes widened. 'Actually, that makes a lot of sense. I should've thought of that. Thank you. Obviously I'll reimburse you for whatever you've paid out.'

'There's no need—it's my van,' he said.

She frowned. 'But this isn't your mess, so why…?'

'Because you're Hugh's sister-in-law,' he said. 'If this had happened to my sister when I was out of the country, Hugh and Tarq would've looked out for her. So I'm doing the same, by extension.'

'Considering that you and I didn't exactly hit it off at the wedding,' she said, 'this is really nice of you. And I appreciate it. Thank you.'

Roland was beginning to think that he'd seriously misjudged Grace. If she'd been the spoiled, princessy drunk he'd thought she was, she would've been wailing and expecting everyone else to sort out the mess for her—most probably while she swigged a glass of wine and wandered about doing nothing. Instead, while he'd been away, she'd been quietly and efficiently getting on with moving stuff out of the flat. Not liking the guilt that was beginning to seep through him, he handed her a brownie. 'Chocolate. My sister says it makes everything better.'

Then she smiled—the first real smile he'd seen from her—and he was shocked to discover that it made the street feel as if it had just lit up.

'Your sister sounds like a wise woman.'

'She is.'

Roland Devereux was the last person Grace had expected to come to her rescue, but she really appreciated the fact that he had. And today he was very different from the way he'd been at the wedding. This time, he didn't make her feel the way that Howard's mother always made her feel. He treated her like a human being instead of something nasty stuck to the bottom of his shoe.

Fortified by the coffee and the brownies, between them they had most of Grace's things outside in boxes and bags by the time Roland's van arrived. And in the meantime, Grace's neighbours had returned, offering sympathy when they saw the mess and thankfully finding the landlord's number for her.

She called the landlord, but there was no answer, so she left a message explaining what had happened and giving him her mobile number, and continued moving stuff out of the flat.

Roland's plumber arrived and took a look at the burst pipe.

'It's very old piping around here,' he said. 'The system probably got blocked somewhere along the line, and this pipe had a weaker joint that couldn't cope with the extra pressure.'

'So it wasn't anything I did wrong?' Grace asked.

'No, love—it was just one of those things. I can do a temporary repair now, and then sort it out properly tomorrow.'

She nodded. 'Thank you. Let me have an invoice and I'll pay you straight away.'

'No need—the boss is covering it.'

'The boss?' she asked, mystified.

'Roland,' the plumber explained.

What? But it shouldn't be Roland's bill. OK. Right now she didn't have time for a discussion. She'd sort it out with him later.

She'd just left the plumber when a restoration specialist turned up and introduced himself. He took photographs of everything, and asked her to hold a metal ruler against the wall to show the depth of the water. 'For the insurance,' he explained. And then he brought a machine from his van to start sucking up the water.

'I really appreciate everything you've done to help me,' Grace said to Roland. 'Just one more thing—do you happen to know the number of a good lock-up place as well?'

He shrugged. 'There's no need. You can store your things at my place.'

She blinked. 'But you don't know me. You only met me once before today. For all you know, I could be a thief or a fraudster.'

He shrugged again. 'You're my best friend's sister-in-law—that's good enough for me.' He paused. 'You really can't stay at the flat until it's dried out properly.'

'I know.' She grimaced. 'Hopefully I can per-suade one of my friends to let me crash on their floor tonight, then I'll find a hotel or something to put me up until the flat's usable again.'

It was a sensible enough plan, and if Roland agreed with her he wouldn't have to get involved.

But something in her expression made him say, 'I have a spare room.'

She shook her head. 'Thank you, but I've al-ready imposed on you far too much.'

'It's getting late,' he said, 'plus your stuff's all in the back of your car, my car, and the van. You can't do anything else here until the landlord calls you back and the insurance assessors turn up—which won't be until at least tomorrow. And you said yourself that none of your friends have the room to put you up, let alone store your stuff as well. So come and stay with me.'

'That's—that's really kind of you.'

He could see her blinking back the tears and lifted his hands in a 'stop' gesture. 'Don't cry. Please.' He didn't cope well with tears. He never had. Which had been half the problem in that last year with Lynette. He'd backed away when he shouldn't have done. And she'd paid the ultimate price.

Grace swallowed back the threatening tears and scrubbed at her eyes with the back of her hand. 'OK. No more tears, I promise. But thank you. I owe you.'

CHAPTER TWO

ONCE THE RESTORATION man had finished getting rid of the worst of the water and Grace had locked the flat, she programmed Roland's address into her satnav in case she got stuck in traffic and lost both him and the van on the way, then followed him back to his house—which turned out to be in a swish part of Docklands. Once she'd parked behind his car, outside what looked like a development of an old maltings, Roland and the van driver helped her transfer her things from their cars and the van to his garage.

'Everything will be safe here for tonight,' he said when they'd finished.

'And dry,' Grace added. 'Thank you.'

There was a row of shops on the ground floor of the building, and Grace assumed that Roland had a flat on one of the upper floors; to her surprise, she discovered that his house was at one end of the building. And when he showed her into the townhouse itself, she saw that the entire back of the house was a glass box extension. It was incredibly modern, but at the same time it didn't feel out of place—and the views over the river were utterly amazing.

'This place is incredible,' she said.

He looked pleased. 'I like it.'

'But—' she gestured to the floor-to-ceiling windows '—no curtains? Don't you worry about people peering in?'

'I have a little bit of trickery instead. It's much cleaner, design-wise. And I loathe frills and flounces—my idea of hell is those swags of fussy fabrics.'

And those were just the kind of thing Grace had in mind for her own dream home—a pretty little Victorian terraced house, with sprigged flowery wallpaper and curtains to match, and lots of cushions in cosy armchairs.

He flicked a switch and the glass became opaque, giving them complete privacy.

'Very clever,' she said. And although she

would've preferred the kind of curtains he hated, she could understand what he liked about it. 'Did you have an architect design this for you?'

'That,' Roland said, 'would be me.'

Grace stared at him in surprise. 'You're an architect?'

He nodded. 'I designed Hugh and Tarquin's offices,' he said, 'and I had a hand in remodelling Hugh's place so it's soundproof—for the sake of his neighbours, if he gets up in the middle of the night and starts composing on the piano.'

'This is amazing.' She shook her head. 'What an idiot I am. I thought you were some sort of builder, given that you had a plumber and a van.'

He smiled. 'You weren't that far off. I'm in the building trade, and I was pretty hands-on with this place. I guess this was my prototype.'

'How do you mean, prototype?' she asked, not understanding.

'My company makes eco-prefab buildings—either extensions or even the whole house. They're all made off site, and they can be put up in a matter of days.'

'You mean, like the ones you see on TV documentaries about people building their own houses or restoring old industrial buildings and turning them into homes?' she asked.

'They've been featured on that sort of programme, yes,' he said.

'That's seriously impressive.'

He inclined his head in acknowledgement of the compliment. 'I enjoy it. Let me show you to the guest room.'

Like the rest of the rooms she'd seen so far, the bedroom was very modern, simply furnished and with little on the walls. But, with one wall being pure glass, she supposed you wouldn't need anything else to look at: not when you had a whole panorama of London life to look at. Water and people and lights and the sky.

There was a king-sized bed with the headboard set in the middle of the back wall, a soft duvet and fluffy pillows. The bed linen was all white— very high maintenance, she thought. The en-suite bathroom was gorgeous, and was about six times the size of the bathroom in Bella's flat; Grace still wasn't quite used to thinking of Bella's old place as her own flat.

She took the bare minimum from her case—it seemed pointless to unpack everything just for one night, when tomorrow she'd be moving to a hotel or whatever alternative accommodation the insurance company offered—and hung her office clothes for the next day in the wardrobe so they wouldn't be creased overnight. Just as she was about to go back downstairs in search of Roland, her phone rang; thankfully, it was the landlord, who'd spoken to the insurance company and could fill her in on what was happening next.

Roland was sitting at the kitchen table, checking his emails on his phone, when Grace walked into the kitchen, looking slightly shy.

'Can I get you a drink?' he asked.

'No, thanks. I'm fine,' she said. 'The landlord just called me. He's talked to the insurance company and they're getting a loss assessor out to see the flat—and me—tomorrow morning at eleven.'

She sounded a little unsure, he thought. 'Is getting the time off work going to be a problem for you?'

She wrinkled her nose. 'I'm temping at the moment—but if I explain the situation and make the hours up, I'm sure they'll be fine about it.'

He was surprised. 'Temping? So you're what, a PA?'

'An accountant,' she corrected.

Which made it even more surprising that she didn't have a permanent job. 'How come you're temping?'

'It's a long and boring story. It's also why I've moved into Bella's flat.' She flapped a hand dismissively. 'But it's not because I'm a criminal or anything, so you don't need to worry about that. I just made some decisions that made life a bit up in the air for me.'

He wondered what those decisions had been. But she was being cagey about it, so he decided not to push it. It was none of his business, in any case. 'You can keep your stuff here as long as you need to, so that isn't a problem.' He glanced at his watch. 'You must be hungry. I certainly am, so I was thinking of ordering us a takeaway.'

'Which I'll pay for,' she said immediately.

'Hardly. You're my guest.'

'You weren't expecting me,' she pointed out.

'And I'd feel a lot happier if you let me pay. It's the least I can do, considering how much you've done for me this evening.'

He could see that she wasn't going to budge on the issue. In her shoes, he'd feel the same way, so he decided to give in gracefully. 'OK. Thank you.'

'And I'm doing the washing up,' she added.

'There's no need. I have a housekeeping service.'

She scoffed. 'I'm still not leaving a pile of dirty dishes next to the sink.'

A princess would've taken a housekeeper for granted. Grace didn't, and she clearly wasn't playing a part. How on earth had he got her so wrong? 'We'll share the washing up,' he said, feeling guilty about the way he'd misjudged her. 'What do you like? Chinese? Pizza?'

'Anything,' she said.

So she wasn't fussy about food, either.

And, given the way she was dressed…it was almost as if she was trying to blend in to her surroundings. Minimum fuss, minimum attention.

Why would someone want to hide like that?

Not that it was any of his business. He ordered a selection of dishes from his local Chinese take-away. 'It'll be here in twenty minutes,' he said when he put the phone down.

It felt very odd to be domesticated, Roland thought as he laid two places at the kitchen table. For nearly two years he'd eaten most of his evening meals alone, except if he'd been on business or when Hugh, Tarquin or his sister Philly had insisted on him joining them. Being here alone with Grace was strange. But he just about managed to make small talk with her until the food arrived.

His hand brushed against hers a couple of times when they heaped their plates from the takeaway cartons, and that weird prickle of awareness he'd felt at the wedding made itself known again.

Did she feel it, too? he wondered. Because she wasn't meeting his eyes, and had bowed her head slightly so her hair covered her face. Did he fluster her, the way she flustered him?

And, if so, what were they going to do about it?

Not that he was really in a position to do anything about it. He'd told Hugh and Tarquin that he was ready to date again, but he knew he wasn't. How could he trust himself not to let a new partner down, given the way he'd let his wife down? Until he could start to forgive himself, he couldn't move on.

'Don't feel you have to entertain me,' she said when they'd finished eating and had sorted out the washing up. 'I've already taken up more than enough of your time this evening, and I don't want to be a demanding house guest. If you don't mind, I'm going to sort out Bella's shoeboxes for her so all her papers are in some sort of order.'

So Grace was the sort who liked organisation and structure. That made it even stranger that she'd call off her wedding only three weeks before the big day. There was a lot more to that story than met the eye, Roland was sure; but he didn't want to intrude on her privacy by asking.

'I'll be in my office next door if you need me. Feel free to make yourself a drink whenever you like. There are tea, coffee and hot chocolate capsules in the cupboard above the coffee machine.' He gestured to the machine sitting on the work surface.

'Thanks.' For the first time, she gave him a teasing smile. 'Now I've seen your house, I'm not surprised you have a machine like that.'

'Are you accusing me of being a gadget fiend?' he asked.

'Are you one?' she fenced back.

He grinned. 'Just a tiny bit—what about you?' The question was out before he could stop it, and he was shocked at himself. Was he actually flirting with her? He couldn't even remember the last time he'd flirted with anyone.

'I use an old-fashioned cafetière and a teapot,' she said. 'Though I might admit to having a milk-frother, because I like cappuccinos.'

Tension suddenly crackled between them. And Roland was even more shocked to find himself wondering what would happen if he closed the gap between them and brushed his mouth very lightly over Grace's.

What on earth was he doing? Apart from the fact that his head was still in an emotional mess, Grace was the last person he should think about kissing. He'd just rescued her from a burst pipe situation. She was as vulnerable as Lyn had been.

He needed to back off. Now. 'See you later,' he said, affecting a cool he most definitely didn't feel, and sauntered into his office.

Though even at the safety of his desk he found it hard to concentrate on his work. Instead of opening the file for his current project, he found himself thinking of a quiet, dark-haired woman with the most amazing cornflower-blue eyes— and he was cross with himself because he didn't want to think about her in that way. Right now he couldn't offer a relationship to anyone. Who knew when he'd be ready to date again—if ever.

Grace sorted through the contents of Bella's shoe-boxes at Roland's kitchen table, putting every-thing in neat piles so she could file them away properly in a binder. She tried to focus on what she was doing, but the mundane task wasn't oc-cupying anywhere near enough of her head for her liking. It left way too much space for her to think about the man who'd unexpectedly come to her rescue.

And now she was seeing Roland Devereux in a whole new light. He'd been cold and taciturn when she'd first met him. She would never have believed that he was a man with vision. A man who could create such a stunning modern design, which somehow didn't feel out of place in its very traditional setting; he'd merged the old and the new perfectly to get the best of both worlds.

She couldn't resist taking a swift break and looking him up on the Internet. And she liked what she saw on his company website, especially the way they paid attention to detail. Although the houses they built were prefabricated, the designs didn't feel as if they were identikit; from the gallery of pictures of the finished houses, Grace could see that Roland's company had added touches to each one to make it personal to the families who'd wanted to build them. And not only was he great at design, he'd worked with conservation officers on several projects. One in particular involved an eco extension that had enhanced the old building it was part of, rather than marring it, and he'd won an award for it.

There was much more to Roland Devereux than met the eye.

And she had to push away the memory of that

moment when he'd flirted with her in the kitchen. Right now, her life was too chaotic for her to consider adding any kind of relationship to the mix. And, although Roland seemed to live alone, for all she knew he could already be committed elsewhere.

So she'd just put this evening down to the kindness of a stranger, and consider herself lucky that her brother-in-law had such a good friend.

Roland had already left for the day when Grace got up the next morning, even though she'd planned to be at her desk by eight. He'd left her his spare door key along with a note on the table asking her to set the house alarm, giving her the code. He'd added, *Call me if any problems.*

She texted him to say that she'd set the alarm and thanked him for the loan of his key, then headed for the office. At work, she explained the situation to her boss, who was kind enough to let her reorganise her work schedule so she could meet the loss assessor at the flat.

But the news from the loss assessor wasn't good. It would take a couple of weeks to dry out the flat, even with dehumidifiers, and there was a chance they might need to take all the plaster off the walls to stop mould developing, and then re-plaster the walls. Which in turn would take time to dry. And the landlord would probably have to look into replacing the plumbing completely in the very near future. And that meant even more disruption.

How could a burst pipe cause so much chaos?

And she could hardly invite herself to stay with Roland for an unforeseeable amount of time. Her parents lived too far out of London for her to be able to commute from their place, and she knew her friends didn't have the room to put her up, so she'd just have to find a room in a budget hotel. Hopefully Roland wouldn't mind her leaving her stuff in his garage for another day or so until she could organise storage.

She called in to a specialist wine shop to buy a thank-you gift for him on her way back to the office, then worked through her lunch hour and left late that evening to make up the time she'd had to take out to meet the assessor. When she returned to the house in Docklands, Roland was in the kitchen, making himself a coffee.

'Hi. Coffee?' he asked, gesturing to the machine.

'Thanks, but I'm fine. Oh, and I got this for you.'

She handed him the bottle bag, and he blinked in surprise. 'What's this?'

'To say thank you,' she said. 'I have no idea if you prefer red or white wine, so I played it safe and bought white.'

'That's very kind of you,' he said.

But she noticed that he hadn't even opened the bag to look at the wine. 'Sorry. Obviously I should've gone for red.'

'Actually, I don't drink,' he said.

Grace wished the ground would open up and swallow her. 'I'm so sorry.' And she wasn't going to ask him why. It was none of her business.

'You weren't to know.' He opened the bag and looked at the label. 'Montrachet is lovely. I know a certain woman who will love you to bits for bringing this.'

His girlfriend? Grace squashed the seeping disappointment. So not appropriate. And it raised another issue. 'I hope your girlfriend doesn't mind me staying.'

'No girlfriend. I was talking about my little sister,' Roland said. 'Just because I don't drink, it doesn't mean that I make everyone else stick to water.'

And the little rush of pleasure at discovering he was single was even more inappropriate. 'Uh-huh,' she said, knowing she sounded awkward, and wishing yet again that she could be as open and spontaneous as her sister.

'So how did it go with the loss assessor?' he asked.

'Not great.' She told him what the loss assessor had said. 'So if you don't mind me staying here again tonight, I'll sort out a hotel room for tomorrow night onwards. I'll find a storage place, and it shouldn't take me too many trips to ferry all my stuff there.'

'Why go to all that trouble when I've already said you can stay in my spare room and store your stuff here?' he asked.

'Because I can't impose on you for an open-ended amount of time,' she explained. 'I know you're my brother-in-law's best friend, but this is way beyond the call of duty, and I'd rather stand on my own two feet.'

'Noted,' he said, 'but you said yesterday that you'd made some choices that made life a bit up in the air for you. I think we all have times like that, when we could maybe use a friend.'

'You're offering to be my friend?'

He looked at her, his dark eyes full of questions, and suddenly there didn't seem to be enough air in the room.

Was he offering her friendship…or something else? She didn't trust her judgement to read the situation properly.

And then Roland said, 'Yes, I think I'm offering to be your friend.'

'But we don't know each other,' she pointed out.

'I know, and I admit I took you the wrong way when I first met you.'

She frowned. 'Meaning?'

He winced. 'Meaning that I've been a bit judgemental and I can see for myself that you're not what I thought you were.'

'You're digging yourself a hole here.'

'Tell me about it,' he said wryly. 'And I'm sorry.'

'So what did you think I was?' she asked.

'Are you sure you want to hear this?'

No, but she'd gone far enough to have to keep up the bravado. 'I wouldn't have asked otherwise.'

'OK. I thought of you as the Runaway Bride,' he said.

He'd thought *what*? Obviously he knew that she'd cancelled her wedding quite late in the day—but he'd assumed that she was some kind of spoiled brat? She narrowed her eyes at him. 'You're right, that's judgemental and that's not who I am—and, for your information, I didn't leave my fiancé at the aisle or even close to it. In fact, I hadn't even bought a wedding dress.'

It was his turn to frown. 'But Hugh said you cancelled the wedding three weeks beforehand. And I've seen by the way you've dealt with the flood that you're organised. This doesn't add up.

Why didn't you have a wedding dress that close to the big day?'

'It's a long and very boring story,' she said.

'I don't have anything better to do—do you?' he asked.

She blew out a breath. 'Maybe, maybe not. And I guess if I'm going to stay with you, you probably need to know why my life's a bit chaotic.'

'Let's talk over pizza,' he said, 'and maybe a glass of wine. We could open this bottle now.'

'You just told me you didn't drink.'

'I also told you I don't make everyone else around me stick to water.'

'I don't actually drink that much,' she admitted.

He looked at her. 'But the first time you met Hugh…'

Oh, no. Well, he was Hugh's best friend. Of course he'd know about what happened. 'I threw up over Hugh because I'd drunk three glasses of champagne on an empty stomach. Which is more than I would usually drink in a month.' Shame flooded through her at the memory. 'Does *everyone* know about that?'

'Tarq and I do.'

'Tarquin never mentioned it when he met me.'

He gave her a wry smile. 'Probably because Tarq's nicer than I am.'

'I'm reserving the right to stay silent.' Because Roland had come to her rescue, and he was offering her a place to stay. But she was still annoyed that he'd thought so badly of her without even waiting to hear her side of the story. Maybe she'd been right in her first impression of him, too, and he was firmly in the same box as Cynthia Sutton: cold, judgemental and obsessed by appearances.

He raised his eyebrows. 'Isn't the rest of that speech along the lines that if you want to rely on something later in court, you have to speak now?'

'Am I on trial?' she asked.

'Of course not.' He shook his head. 'Pizza it is, then. And mineral water.'

'Provided I pay for the pizza. I don't want you thinking I'm a freeloader as well as being the Runaway Bride and a lush to boot.'

The slight colour staining his cheeks told her that was exactly what he'd thought of her. Which was totally unfair—he'd jumped to conclusions without even knowing her. If it wasn't for the fact that he'd come to her rescue last night and been kind, right at that moment she would've disliked him even more than she had at the wedding.

'I know now that you're none of those things. And you insisted on paying last night, so this is on me,' he said.

'If you buy the pizza,' she said, still cross that he thought she was one of life's takers, 'then I want an invoice for the use of your van yesterday.'

'How about,' he suggested, 'we go halves on the pizza?'

She folded her arms. 'I'd prefer to pay.'

He met her glare head-on. 'Halves or starve. That's the choice.'

And how tempted she was to choose the latter. On principle. Except she was really, really hungry and it was pointless spiting herself. 'OK. Halves. But I do the washing up. And, tomorrow, I cook for us.'

'You can cook?' He looked taken aback.

She could guess why. 'I love my little sister to bits,' she said, 'but Bella's a bit of a disaster in the kitchen. If she's cooked for you, then I understand why you're surprised—but her culinary skills don't run in the family.'

'She hasn't cooked for me. But Hugh told me how bad her stir-fry is,' he admitted.

'In her defence, she does make great pancakes and cupcakes.'

He smiled. 'But you can't live on pancakes and cupcakes alone.'

'Exactly. Is there anything you don't eat, or do you have any food intolerances or allergies?'

'No—and you can use anything you like in the kitchen.'

'I'm glad you said that, because your kitchen is gorgeous and it'll be a pleasure to cook here.' She gestured round. 'So do I take it that you're a cook, too, or is this just for show?'

Roland thought back to the times when he and Lynette had cooked together. Never in this kitchen—he'd still been renovating the place when the drunk driver had smashed into his wife's car. And he hadn't had the heart to cook since. Most of the time he lived on sandwiches, takeaways or microwaved supermarket meals; apart from when his family and his best friends insisted on seeing him, he filled the time with work, work and more work, so he didn't have the space to think. 'I don't cook much nowadays,' he said.

'Fair enough.' To his relief, she didn't pry.

'But if you can text me and let me know what time you want to eat tomorrow,' she added, 'that would be helpful.'

'I'll do that,' he said. Though it felt weirdly domestic, and it made him antsy enough not to press Grace about the reason why she'd moved to Bella's flat—just in case she expected him to share about his past, too. The last thing he wanted was for her to start pitying him—the poor widower who'd lost his wife tragically young. Especially because he didn't deserve the pity. He hadn't taken enough care of Lyn, and he'd never forgive himself for that.

Grace's phone pinged. 'I'm expecting something. Can I be rude and check my phone?' she asked.

'Be my guest.'

She glanced at the screen and smiled. 'Oh, I like this. Today's Bellagram is the Golden Gate Bridge,' she said, showing him the photograph of Bella and Hugh posing with the iconic bridge behind them.

'Bellagram?' Roland asked, not quite understanding.

'Postcard. Telegram—the modern version,' Grace explained. 'Bella likes puns.'

'She texts you every day?'

Grace nodded. 'We always text each other if we're away, sending a photo of what we've been doing. Bella forgot about the time difference for the first one, so it woke me at three in the morning.' She laughed. 'But that's Bella for you. It's great to know they're having a good time.'

'Have you told her about…?'

'The flood? No. I don't want her worrying. I just text her back to say I'm glad she's having fun and I love her,' Grace said.

Which was pretty much what his own family had done when he and Lyn had sent a couple of brief texts from the rainforest on their honeymoon, purely to stop everyone at home worrying that they'd got lost or been eaten by piranhas. Another surge of guilt flooded through him. He'd taken care of Lyn then. Where had it all gone so wrong?

He was glad when Grace was tactful enough to switch the subject to something neutral and kept the conversation easy.

Though later that evening Roland still couldn't get her out of his head. He lay awake, watching the sky through the glass ceiling of his bedroom—a ceiling that wasn't overlooked by anyone or anything—and thinking of her.

What was it about Grace Faraday?

He'd misjudged her completely. Far from being a spoiled, princessy drunk, Grace was a capable and quietly organised woman with good manners. She was a little bit shy, very independent, and *nice*. Easy to be with.

Which was why he probably ought to find somewhere else for her to stay. Grace Faraday was dangerous to his peace of mind. She was the first woman in a long time to intrigue him. Or attract him. And for someone like her to call off a wedding only three weeks before the ceremony… Something had to have been very wrong indeed. Even though it was none of his business, he couldn't help wondering. Had she discovered some really serious character flaw in her husband-to-be?

She'd been going to tell him about it, and then they'd been sidetracked. Maybe she'd tell him tomorrow.

And maybe that would be the thing to keep his common sense in place and stop him doing something stupid.

Like acting on the strong pull he felt towards her and actually kissing her.

CHAPTER THREE

THE FOLLOWING EVENING, Roland opened his front door and stopped dead. It was strange to smell dinner cooking; he could definitely smell lemons, and possibly fish.

Then he realised he could also hear music; clearly Grace had connected her MP3 player to his speakers in the kitchen. Odd; he'd half expected her to like very formal classical music, but right now she was playing vintage feel-good pop songs. And she was singing along. He smiled as she launched into 'Build Me Up, Buttercup', ever so slightly out of key.

But were the song lyrics a warning to him that she didn't want her heart broken? Not that he should be thinking about a relationship with her anyway. His smile faded as he went into the kitchen. 'Good evening, Grace.'

'Oh! Roland. Hello.' She looked up from whatever she was doing and smiled at him, and to his shock his heart felt as if it had done a somersault.

When had he last reacted to someone like this?

Then her face went bright red as she clearly thought about what she'd been doing when he'd opened his front door. 'Um—I apologise for the singing. I'm afraid I can't hold a tune.'

'That's not a problem,' he reassured her. 'You can sing in the kitchen if you like—though actually I had you pegged for a classical music fiend.'

'The boring accountant who likes boring stuff?' she asked with a wry smile.

'Not all classical music is boring. Have you ever heard Hugh play Bach on the piano? It's amazing stuff.'

'No—and, actually, I do like classical music. Not the super-heavy operatic stuff, though,' she said. 'I've always wanted to go to one of those evenings where they play popular classical music to a background of fireworks.' She paused. 'Not that you want to be bored by my bucket list. Dinner will be about another ten minutes.'

Why did Grace think she was boring? Though

Roland wasn't sure how to ask her, because she seemed to have gone back into her shell. Clearly she was used to being the shy, quiet older sister, while Bella was the bubbly one. He fell back on a polite, 'Something smells nice.'

'Thank you. I wasn't sure if you'd prefer to eat in the dining room or the kitchen, so I guessed that here would be OK—though I can move it if you like.' She gestured to the kitchen table by the glass wall, which she'd set for two.

It was definitely less intimate than his dining room would be, he thought with relief. He wasn't sure if he could handle being in intimate surroundings with her, at least not until he'd got these weird, wayward feelings under control. 'The kitchen's fine,' he said. 'Is there anything I can do to help?'

'Everything's pretty much done,' she said. 'Can I get you a coffee or something?'

'It's fine. I'll make it,' he said. 'Do you want one?'

'That'd be nice.' She smiled at him and went back to scooping the flesh and seeds out of passion fruit. 'Thank you.'

This felt dangerously domesticated, working in the kitchen alongside her. Roland made the coffee in near silence, partly because he didn't have a clue what to say to Grace. His social skills outside work had really atrophied. Right now, he felt as gauche as a schoolboy.

'How was your day?' she asked.

'Fine. How was yours?'

'As exciting as any temporary accountancy job can be,' she said with a smile.

'Are you looking for something permanent?'

She went still. 'Roland, if you're just about to offer me a job out of pity, please don't. I'm perfectly capable of finding myself a job.'

'Actually, I don't have anything right now that would match your skill set,' he said. 'But if I did and I offered you an interview, then I'd expect you to be better than any of the other candidates before I offered you the job.'

'Good,' she said. 'And I guess it was a bit previous of me to jump to the conclusion that you were going to offer me a job—but you've already rescued me this week and...' Her voice trailed off and she looked awkward. 'Sorry.'

'And sometimes rescuers don't know when to stop and let someone stand on their own two feet. I get it,' he said. 'And no offence taken.'

'Thank you. Actually, I did have a job interview the other day. And I think it went well.' She wrinkled her nose. 'But then I came home to find myself flooded out, so I haven't really thought about it since then.' She shrugged. 'I probably haven't got the job, or I would've heard by now.'

'That depends on how many they're interviewing,' Roland said.

'I guess.' She brought a jug of what looked like sparkling elderflower cordial over to the table, and then two plates. 'I thought we could have fig, mozzarella and prosciutto skewers to start.'

'Impressive,' he said.

She laughed. 'There's nothing impressive about threading things onto skewers.'

'It's nicely presented, anyway.' He took a taste. 'And it's a good combination.'

She inclined her head in acknowledgement of the compliment. 'Thank you.'

The citrus-glazed baked salmon with sweet potato wedges, caramelised lemons, spinach and baby carrots was even nicer. 'Now this you did have to cook. Don't tell me this isn't impressive.'

'Again, it's much simpler than it looks. I was kind of guinea-pigging you,' she confessed.

'Guinea-pigging?'

'I'm going to teach Bel to cook,' she said. 'So the food needs to look pretty—but it also has to take minimum effort and not involve planning the cooking time for more than two things at once.'

He smiled at her. 'You're obviously a foodie—so why are you an accountant rather than, say, running your own restaurant?'

Because numbers were safe.

Though Grace didn't quite want to admit that. 'I was good at maths when I was at school, and accountancy has good employment prospects,' she said. 'Plus that way I could study for my qualifications in the evenings while I earned money, rather than ending up with a pile of student debt. It made sense to choose accountancy as my career.' And that was who she was. The sensible, quiet older sister who was good at sorting things out.

'Do you enjoy your job?'

She smiled. 'Bella always groans and says she doesn't get why, but actually I do—I like the patterns in numbers, and the way everything works out neatly.' She paused. 'What about you? Why did you become an architect?'

'Because I love buildings,' he said simply. 'Everything from the simplest rural cottage through to grand Rococo palaces.'

She looked at him. 'I can imagine you living in a grand Rococo palace.'

He smiled. 'They're not all they're cracked up to be. They're very cold in winter.'

She blinked. 'So you've stayed in one?'

'The French side of the family owns a chateau or two,' he admitted.

She felt her eyes widen. 'Your family owns *castles*?' Roland had a posh accent, but she hadn't realised just how posh he was. Way, way outside her own social circle.

'Chateaux tend to go hand in hand with vineyards, and our French family produces wine,' he said. 'Christmas in France when I was young was always magical, because there was always

the most enormous Christmas tree with a silver star on the top, and there were roaring open
fires where you could roast chestnuts and toast
crumpets.'

Now she knew he was teasing her. 'Since when
do they eat crumpets in France?'

He spread his hands. 'What can I say? We tend
to mix the traditions a bit in my family, so we
get the best of both worlds. But, seriously, that
was probably where the architecture stuff started.
Apart from the fact that I liked the lines and the
shapes of the buildings and I was always drawing them as a boy, waking up in a freezing cold
bedroom with ice on the inside of the windows
made me think about how it could be made better. How we could have all the modern conve-
niences we were used to in London, but without
damaging the heritage side of the building.'

'And that's how come you're so good at mix-
ing the old and the new,' she said. 'The front of
your house is an old maltings, but the back half
is as modern as it gets.'

'All the new stuff is eco,' he said, 'and all the old
building is maintained properly.' He shrugged.

'Perhaps I'm greedy, but I like having the best of both worlds. All the comfort and convenience of the modern stuff, and the sheer beauty of the old.'

She smiled and brought over dessert—passion fruit cream with almond *cantuccini*.

'This is seriously nice,' he said.

'Thank you.'

When they'd finished eating, he made them some more coffee.

'You were going to tell me yesterday,' he said, 'why your life got turned upside down. It's a bit unexpected for someone who likes order and structure to make a decision that makes everything messy.'

This time, he didn't sound judgemental, and Grace felt comfortable enough with him to tell him. 'I don't like myself very much for what I did. I know I hurt Howard and I feel bad about that.' She grimaced. 'But if I'd married him it would've been so much worse.'

'For what it's worth,' he said, 'I've already worked out that you're not a spoiled princess. Not even close. So that must've been a serious case of cold feet.'

She nodded. 'If I'm honest, I'd been feeling that way for quite a while, but I thought I could still go through with it.'

'So what happened to change your mind?'

She took a deep breath. 'The Fifty Shades of Beige party.'

Roland almost choked on his coffee. Had he just heard right? 'The *what*?'

'Howard—my ex—it was his parents' golden wedding anniversary,' Grace explained. 'I wasn't looking forward to the party, and Bella drew me this cartoon to make me laugh. She called it "Fifty Shades of Beige".'

He smiled. 'From what Tarq says about her, I can just see Bella doing that.'

'Except the awful thing was that she was right,' Grace said. 'I was the only woman there not wearing beige.'

'And it was a problem?' he asked.

'Not for me. For… Well.' She grimaced. 'Don't get me wrong—I did love Howard. But that's when I finally realised that I wasn't in love with him.'

'And there's a difference?'

'A very big difference,' she said. 'It wasn't fair to marry him, knowing that I didn't love him enough—I didn't love him the way he deserved to be loved. I think we were each other's safe option. We were settling for each other instead of looking for what we really wanted.'

'Why did you need a safe option?' He only realised he'd spoken the question aloud when he saw her wince. 'Sorry. That was intrusive and you don't have to answer,' he said hastily.

'No, it's fine. Just don't tell Bella any of this, OK?'

He frowned. From the way Grace talked, she was clearly very close to her sister. 'Why doesn't Bella know?'

'Because,' Grace said, 'she's my little sister and I love her, and I don't want to burden her with it. Basically, my dad's really unreliable and I didn't want to be like my mum. I wanted my partner to be someone I could trust.'

Roland frowned. 'But I met Ed at the wedding—he seemed really nice and not at all unreliable.'

'Ed is utterly lovely. He's Bella's biological dad,

but he's my stepdad and he adopted me after he married Mum,' Grace explained. 'I think of him as my real dad, and he's been a better father to me than my biological dad could ever have been. But the first time round my mum married a charming man who let her down over and over again. He was terrible with money and he never kept his promises. He hardly ever turned up when he'd promised to be there to see me. We've pretty much lost touch over the years. I just wanted to avoid making my mum's mistake.'

'And in the process you made your own mistake,' he said. 'Picking someone who was reliable but not right for you.'

She nodded. 'Howard's a nice man. He's kind and gentle.'

'But?'

'But he made me feel like part of the furniture, and I probably did the same to him,' she admitted. 'I never once felt swept off my feet. And I think we both secretly had doubts—after all, we were engaged for four years.'

In the twenty-first century, that was an unusually long engagement, Roland thought. 'Were you saving up for a house?'

'Avoiding it, I think, if I'm honest,' Grace said. 'We didn't even live together. And if we'd really loved each other, the wedding and everything else wouldn't have mattered—we would've been together regardless. But we weren't.' She dragged in a breath. 'The truth is, if I'd married Howard, his mother would've run our lives—right down to the tiniest detail.'

'Ah, the old cliché—the interfering mother-in-law.'

'Sadly,' Grace said drily, 'in this case Cynthia more than lived up to the cliché. She wanted us to get married on her fiftieth wedding anniversary, and she wasn't very pleased when I said that I thought she ought to be the centre of attention on her special day rather than having to share it with her son's wedding.'

So Grace was tactful and kind, too, Roland thought. Rather than throw a hissy fit at the idea of sharing her wedding day, she'd tried to make the older woman feel important.

'And,' Grace added, 'I wanted my sister to be my bridesmaid.'

Roland blinked in surprise. 'She didn't want Bella to be a bridesmaid?'

'Cynthia didn't like Bella. She said Bel was too headstrong and too quirky.'

'Bella's a free spirit, yes—and she's great,' Roland said. 'I'm beginning to dislike your almost-mother-in-law.'

'Bella didn't like Cynthia, either. She called her "Mrs Concrete Hair".'

'Because it was never out of place?' Roland had to stifle a grin.

Grace nodded. 'Cynthia prided herself on always being turned out immaculately. And she wore a lot of beige.'

'Did you like her?' he asked.

Grace wrinkled her nose. 'Do I have to answer that?'

'Yes.'

She smiled wryly. 'I think Cynthia and I didn't meet each other's expectations. I wanted a mother-in-law who's like my own mum—someone who's warm and supportive, who'd be there if I needed help, but who would always encourage me to stand on my own two feet. Someone I could be friends with and who'd make me feel part of the family.'

Roland thought of his own parents. That summed up their relationship with Lynette—and his own with Lynette's parents. He'd assumed that was completely normal, but maybe they'd both been lucky.

'And what did Cynthia want?' he asked.

Grace looked away. 'Someone who'd keep up appearances at all times and do whatever she told them to.'

'Which doesn't sound like much fun.'

'It wasn't,' Grace said, her voice so quiet that he could barely hear her. 'I hated being judged all the time, and always falling short.'

Which was what he'd done to her. No wonder she'd been so prickly with him, at first.

And now he was beginning to understand her. Grace was the quiet, sensible sister. The one who'd thought she'd wanted her partner to be completely the opposite of her unreliable father.

And yet what she'd really wanted was to be swept off her feet…

An idea was forming in his head.

A really crazy idea.

But maybe it could work. Could he ask her?

Should he ask her?

'Obviously cancelling the wedding shook up your life a bit,' he said, 'but why did it mean that you became a temp and you taking over the lease of Bella's flat?'

'Because I worked for Howard's family's accountancy practice,' she said. 'I could hardly keep working there when I'd just cancelled my wedding to the boss's son. I couldn't ask them for a reference, in the circumstances, so temping was my only real option. Plus I'd already given notice to my landlord, and he'd leased my flat to someone else.'

So cancelling the wedding had cost Grace her job and her home, too. Now he understood what she meant about a decision turning her life upside down. And it was a decision she clearly hadn't made lightly.

'So what are you looking for, Grace?' he asked carefully. 'Marriage?'

'Maybe, maybe not. I've just come out of a long relationship, and I guess right now I need to find out who I am and think about what I really want.' She wrinkled her nose. 'I just wanted to be swept off my feet once in a while. Which I know isn't going to happen, because I'm very ordinary—I'm not free-spirited and brave like Bella is.'

The crazy idea suddenly seemed that little bit less crazy. Maybe Grace—quiet, sensible Grace—could help him move on, haul him out of the limbo where he'd spent two long years. 'What if you had the chance to be swept off your feet? Would you take it?' he asked.

'That's *really* not going to happen,' Grace said. 'I have friends who've joined online dating sites or gone speed-dating, and they've all ended up disappointed.'

'What if,' he asked carefully, 'the date was with someone you know?'

'Such as?'

'Me.'

'You?' She stared at him, looking shocked. 'But you don't even like me.'

'I was obnoxious to you at the wedding because I'd jumped to some very wrong conclusions about you,' Roland said. 'I've got to know you better over the last couple of days and I've realised how wrong I was. And I apologise for that.'

'Thank you. I think.' She frowned. 'You're actually suggesting that we should date?'

'That we should help each other out,' he corrected. 'You want to be swept off your feet, and I need to practise my dating skills.'

She frowned. 'Why do you need to practise your dating skills?'

Grace had been brave enough to tell him about her life. Roland guessed he owed it to her to be brave back. 'I assume Bella didn't tell you?'

'Tell me what?'

'That my wife was killed in a car accident nearly two years ago—a year before I moved in here.'

She reached across the table and took his hand briefly, squeezing it gently for just long enough to convey sympathy, then letting his hand go before the contact dissolved into pity. 'I didn't know her, and it's a horrible cliché, but I'm really sorry you had to go through losing someone you loved like that.'

'It was hard,' he said. 'And I miss Lynette. A lot.' Mostly. Apart from the one sticking point in their marriage—the thing that had made him jump at the chance to get away for a few days and be rid of all the pressure. And he still felt guilty about it, even though he knew that the accident hadn't been his fault. But part of him still felt that if he'd been here instead of a couple of thousand miles away, maybe Lynette wouldn't have gone out in the car, and she wouldn't have been hit by the drunk driver. Or, even if the accident had still happened, at least he would've been by her side when she'd died, later that night.

He pushed the thought away. 'But missing her won't bring her back—and there isn't such a thing as a time machine, so I can't go back and change the past. Though, if I could, I'd stop the other driver from guzzling her way through a bottle of wine and several cocktails and then getting behind the wheel of her car.'

* * *

Now Grace understood why Roland didn't drink—and why his house was immaculate but didn't feel quite like a home. Because he'd lost the love of his life to the selfish actions of a drunk driver. 'That's so sad,' she said.

He said nothing, but gave a small nod of acknowledgement.

'But I still don't get why you're asking *me* to help you practise your dating skills.'

He reached across the table and took her hand, then drew it up to his mouth and pressed a kiss into her palm.

And Grace tingled all over. Nobody had ever kissed her hand like that before.

'My friends,' he said, 'and my family have tried to find me someone suitable to heal my broken heart.'

'Too soon?'

'Partly,' he agreed. 'But I know Lyn wouldn't have wanted me to spend the rest of my life on my own, mourning her. She would've wanted me to share my life with someone who loves me as much as she did.'

For a moment, a shadow crossed his expression. It was gone before she could be sure it was there. Maybe she'd imagined it, because hadn't he just pretty much told her that Lynette was the love of his life? Or maybe that shadow had been grief that he was still trying to be brave about.

'So,' he said, 'I'm going to start dating again. Put my life back together. But I'm finding it hard.'

'Because you're not ready to move on?'

He dragged in a breath. 'And I'm out of practice. I need to date someone who won't mind if I make mistakes and will help me get better at dating. And you want to be swept off your feet, just for a little while. So that's why perhaps we can help each other out. For two weeks.'

'Until Bella and Hugh are back from honeymoon. And no strings?' she checked.

'No strings. We could just clear our diaries outside work for those two and a bit weeks and spend time together.'

'Like a holiday?'

'I guess,' he said.

A holiday with the best man. Part of Grace wanted to say yes; but part of her wondered just how sensible this was. Roland Devereux wasn't the surly, barely civil man she'd met at Bella's wedding. He was kind and sensitive—and this side of him was seriously attractive. But he still had a broken heart; and, even though he thought he wanted to try looking for love again, that made him vulnerable.

She knew that she was vulnerable, too. Her life was still all up in the air. She wanted to stand on her own two feet and work out what she wanted from life. And did she really want to take the risk of dating someone who wasn't going to be available and maybe falling in love with him? Or would this be the thing that changed her life and made everything right again? 'Can I have some time to think about it?' she asked.

'Of course. Maybe you could tell me your answer tomorrow?'

'All right.' Sitting here at the kitchen table with him didn't feel casual and easy any more; Grace felt hot and bothered, remembering the touch of his mouth against her skin. For the last four years—and for longer than that, if she was honest—she hadn't felt anything like this. Like a teenager about to go on her first date, with her heart pattering away and butterflies dancing a tango in her stomach. 'I'd better do the washing up,' she said, taking the coward's way out of facing him.

'I'll help.'

Which would put them at even closer range. She couldn't risk that. 'There's no need,' she said brightly.

'There's every need,' he corrected. 'It's my kitchen—and I'm not the kind to make other people do my share of the chores.'

She had no answer to that.

But, as they worked by the sink, they ended up brushing against each other. Grace tingled all over—which was ridiculous, because they were both fully clothed and, technically speaking, his shirtsleeve had touched her dress, which was nothing like his bare arm against her bare torso.

And then she really wished she hadn't thought of that, because now she was imagining what it would be like if Roland was skin to skin with her.

She went very still, and looked at him. He was exactly the same: still and watchful. So had he felt that strange connection between them? Was he tingling all over, too?

Grace couldn't help glancing at Roland's mouth. His lips were slightly parted, revealing even, white teeth; how had she not noticed before how sensual the curve of his mouth was? When she looked up again, she realised that he was looking at her mouth, too.

And then he leaned forward and kissed her. It was the lightest, gentlest, most unthreatening brush of his mouth against hers, and it sent shards of desire all through her. She couldn't ever remember a kiss making her feel as hot and shivery as this before.

'Tell me tomorrow,' he whispered.

She shook her head. 'I can give you the answer right now.' Even though part of her knew this was crazy and she ought to be measured and sensible about this, the way she always was, a stronger part of her couldn't resist the challenge. And maybe taking a leaf out of Bella's book—living life to the full, instead of being sensible all the time and holding back—would be good for her.

Two weeks. No strings.

Time to take the leap.

'Yes.'

CHAPTER FOUR

THE MIDDLE OF the next morning, Roland texted Grace.

Do you have a posh cocktail dress?

She thought about it. Was he planning to take her to a cocktail bar or something? Given that Roland was six-foot-two, she could actually wear her one pair of high heels without being taller than he was and making him feel embarrassed. She could team them with a little black dress, and maybe put her hair up.

Yes. Why?

Taking you out for dinner tonight. Need you to be ready for seven. Does that fit in OK for work?

Which meant she had absolutely no idea where they were going; all she knew was that the dress code meant posh. It could be anything from a private dinner party in a castle somewhere—given that Roland's family owned chateaux in France and he mixed in very different circles from her own—to dinner at Claridge's. Was this what it felt like to be swept off your feet, not having a clue about what was happening? Grace was used to being organised and in charge, and right now she felt a bit out of her depth. But she brazened it out.

Sure, can be ready.

Good. Any allergies or things you can't bear to eat?

No to both.

Excellent. See you at seven.

Where are we going? she texted, though she had a feeling that he wouldn't tell her.

Out, was the reply that she'd half expected, leaving her none the wiser.

Roland wasn't at the house when Grace went back to Docklands after work. But he'd asked her to be ready for seven, so she showered, changed and did her hair to make sure she'd be ready. As she started applying her make-up, a wave of nervousness swept through her. This was their 'date'—and it had put her in a complete spin. She knew this wasn't a real relationship, but Roland had promised to sweep her off her feet, and she'd promised to let him practise his dating skills.

Did that mean he was going to kiss her again? And those feelings she'd had last night—would they get to the point of overwhelming her common sense? Would she end up making a fool of herself?

She tried to put the thought from her mind and concentrated on getting ready. By the time she'd finished, it was ten to seven and Roland still hadn't come back from work. Given that he'd asked her to be ready for seven, if he turned up in the next few seconds it wouldn't leave him much time to get ready to go out. But surely if he'd been held up at work or in traffic he would've called her?

Had she just made a huge mistake and agreed to a ridiculous deal with someone who would turn out to be as unreliable as her father? Someone charming who would let her down? That would mean she'd gone from one extreme to the other: from thinking of marrying a sensible man who didn't make her heart beat faster, to dating one who'd break it without a second thought. That wasn't what she wanted. At all.

Maybe she should call the whole thing off and find herself somewhere else to stay until Bella's flat had dried out.

She was about to start looking up hotels when the doorbell rang. Even though it wasn't strictly her place to answer the door, maybe it was a delivery or neighbour who needed something and she really ought to answer. When she opened the door, she saw Roland standing on the doorstep. He smiled and handed her a single red rose. 'Hi.'

'Thank you,' she said. Then she noticed the way he was dressed. He was wearing a formal dinner jacket, with a bow tie—and she was pretty sure that wasn't what he'd normally wear to the office. 'But—but...'

'But what?' he asked, his dark eyes glittering;

clearly he was enjoying the fact that she was completely wrong-footed.

She gestured to his suit. 'You didn't come back here to get changed.'

'I can hardly sweep you off your feet if you see all the domestic stuff first,' he pointed out with a grin. 'I came home at lunchtime to pick up my clothes and I got changed in the office.'

'Oh.' Feeling stupid and vaguely pathetic, Grace stared at the floor. Why hadn't she thought of that? And that was why he was here at pre-cisely seven o'clock—the time when he'd asked her to be ready. Of course he wasn't unreliable. She'd jumped to conclusions and been as unfair to him as he'd been to her.

Roland reached out, gently put the backs of his fingers under her chin and tilted her chin until she met his gaze. 'Hey. This was meant to make you feel special, not awkward,' he said. 'But I did warn you my dating skills are rusty. I'm sorry I got it wrong.'

If this was Roland in rusty mode, heaven help her when he was polished. 'It's not you, it's me being stupid,' she mumbled. 'I'd better put this rose in water—and it's lovely. Thank you.' And now she was babbling like a fool. He must be really regretting making that deal with her.

As if he could read her mind, he said quietly, 'Grace, just *relax*. This is about having fun.' Then he leaned forward and brushed his lips very lightly against hers, which sent her into even more of a tizzy. Every nerve end in her lips tingled and her knees felt as if they'd turned to soup.

'You have two minutes,' he said.

She just about managed to get her head together enough to ask, 'Where do you keep your vases?'

'Um—I don't have any, which is a bit pathetic given that my sister Philly is a florist.' He flapped a hand dismissively. 'Just use a glass for now and we'll sort it out later.'

The momentary confusion on his face made her feel a bit better. She put the rose in a glass of water in the kitchen, then joined him again at the front door.

'Your transport awaits, madam.'

She had no idea what she'd been expecting—but it certainly wasn't the gleaming silver Rolls-

Royce that waited for them by the kerb, with a chauffeur at the wheel wearing a peaked cap.

'A Rolls-Royce?' she asked.

'In design terms, I prefer this to a stretch limo,' he said with a grin, and helped her into the car.

'Are you quite sure your dating skills need polishing, Roland?' she asked when he joined her in the back of the car. 'Because I think you've already swept me off my feet tonight more than I've ever been swept in my entire life so far.'

He inclined his head in acknowledgement. 'Good. That's the plan.'

They stopped outside a restaurant in Mayfair. The chauffeur opened the passenger door for her, and then Roland was by her side, tucking her arm into his elbow and leading her to the restaurant.

Grace recognised the name of the place as one of the best restaurants in London. It had two Michelin stars and the food was legendary—and it was so far out of her budget that she'd never even dreamed of booking a table here for a special birthday. Yet she noticed that the *maître d'* greeted Roland as if he was very well known here, then ushered them over to an intimate table for two.

She drank in her surroundings. This was definitely a once in a lifetime opportunity. The room was very light and airy, and was decorated in Regency style. There were Venetian glass chandeliers suspended from the ceiling, with beautiful art in gilded frames and a huge antique mirror hanging on the duck-egg-blue walls. The carpet was in a slightly darker shade than the walls, and her feet actually sank into it as she walked. The dark wood chairs had blue-and-cream-striped seats; the tables were covered with plain white damask cloths and were set with silver cutlery, with a simple arrangement of roses and a candelabrum in the centre.

'This is amazing,' she whispered when the *maître d'* had seated her and left them to look at the wine menu, 'but don't you have to book a table here months in advance?'

'Usually,' Roland agreed with a smile.

Which meant there was a reason why Roland had been able to book a table at the last minute.

'So did you go to school with the owner or something?' she asked.

He shrugged. 'I just did a little bit of renovation work for them, about four years ago.'

'They have one of your glass boxes here?'

'Sadly not. Though I do like the idea of a glass wall between the restaurant and the kitchen so the customers can see their food being cooked,' he said. 'Possibly not for here, though, because it wouldn't work with the architecture. I've booked the tasting menu for us, by the way. I hope that's OK?'

'More than OK, thank you. I've always wanted to do something like this,' she said shyly.

'And don't feel that you have to stick to water just because I don't drink,' he added. 'I'm perfectly happy for you to have the paired wines with each course if you'd like them.'

'I don't drink a lot,' she said, 'so it'd probably be a waste for me to do that. Maybe I could have one glass of wine, if they can recommend something?'

He spoke to the sommelier, who returned with a single glass of champagne and a bottle of water.

'Thank you,' she said quietly. 'That's really lovely.'

'What I like about this place is the attention to detail,' Roland said. 'Maybe it's the architect in me, but I like the fact they've kept the Regency styling right down to the glassware.'

She looked at the glass; the stem was sturdy and the bowl was conical, with an engraving of wine leaves just below the rim. 'This is an antique glass?'

'Reproduction—but a good one,' he said.

The waiter brought out the *amuse bouche*—a sunflower seed crisp with a braised artichoke and a bay leaf cream. Grace had never seen anything so beautifully presented; it looked more like a work of art than a dish.

But the first mouthful was even more amazing; the combination of the tastes, the textures and the scent stunned her.

'I've never had food this good before,' she said in almost hushed tones. 'The way the whole thing is put together and presented—it's incredible.'

Roland looked pleased. 'I hoped you'd enjoy this, seeing as you're a foodie.'

'Hey, I'm strictly amateur,' she said ruefully. 'But I like this very much indeed. Thank you so much for bringing me here.'

He smiled. 'That's what tonight's about, doing something we both like. It's nice to come here with someone I know will get this as much as I do.'

Grace wondered, had Lynette not liked this sort of thing? But she didn't ask; it was too intrusive and might spoil Roland's enjoyment of the evening. And Grace was determined to enjoy being swept off her feet, because she knew she'd never eat at a place like this again. Roland's world was in a completely different league from her own.

Course after course followed, all cooked to perfection and plated beautifully. The staff were friendly and attentive without being over the top, and Grace started to lose her shyness and relax with Roland.

'I hope you've got stamina,' he said with a grin. 'There are eight courses.'

'Eight? That's *so* greedy.' But she grinned back. 'Bring it on. I love everything about this. And, as you say, it's nice to do something like this with someone who gets it.'

'So what else do you like doing?' he asked.

She thought about it. 'Curling up on the sofa with a good book, walking in the park, going to the cinema with friends, and dance aerobics class with Bella. You?'

He considered it. 'I probably spend too much time at work. But I like wandering round museums. Especially ones in gorgeous buildings.'

'Where you look at the architecture and think what you'd do if you were given a free hand?'

'Busted,' he said with a grin.

Grace found herself relaxing with Roland, chatting easily about the food. 'A pre-dessert dessert? What a fabulous idea,' she said when the waiter brought a terrine with lemon verbena cream layered with orange curd, and served with the lightest and crispest almond *tuile*. Even better was the dark chocolate *pavé* with fresh blueberries and shards of dark chocolate. And then there was the cheeseboard, with a selection of cheese, tiny crackers, walnuts and black grapes, all served on a long slate board.

'That was utter perfection,' she said with a sigh. 'And right now I feel like a princess. A very greedy, full-to-bursting one, but definitely a princess.'

'Good.' Roland smiled at her. 'I'm glad you're enjoying this.'

While they had coffee and *petits fours*, the chef came out to see them.

'Ro. It's been too long,' he said, clapping Roland on the shoulder. 'And this is…?'

'Grace Faraday, my friend,' Roland said. 'Grace, this is Max Kleinman.'

'Delighted.' Max shook her hand warmly.

Max Kleinman was the equivalent of a rock star in the culinary world, and Grace felt incredibly shy. She knew Bella would've been in her element here and chatted away to him, and not for the first time she wished she had her sister's people skills. But she was the one who was quiet and sensible and good with numbers. All she could think of to say was, 'Your food is amazing.'

To her relief, Max looked pleased rather than embarrassed. 'I'm glad you liked it. I hope this means you'll come back.'

In my dreams, Grace thought, but she smiled.
'I hope so, too.'

Finally, the Rolls-Royce took them back to Roland's house. Grace was shocked to realise that
it was almost midnight; they'd spent nearly four
hours at the restaurant. She'd never lingered that
long over a meal before.

Roland gestured to his coffee machine. 'Decaf
cappuccino?'

'I think I'm too full to eat for another week,
let alone drink coffee now,' Grace said. 'Thank
you, but I'm fine.'

'So was it OK?' Roland asked.

'More than OK. I've never eaten such amazing
food in my life,' she said. 'Thank you so much
for spoiling me.'

'My pleasure,' he said, sounding utterly sincere
rather than being polite.

'Though I have to be honest,' she said. 'I do
feel as if I'm cheating you. The deal is that I'm
supposed to help you brush up your dating skills
while you're sweeping me off my feet, but as far
as I can see you don't need any help with your
dating skills at all.'

'I think that's because of you,' he said. 'You made me feel comfortable enough to be myself with you. You're easy to talk to. Maybe—I don't know—maybe next time you can be a bit awkward with me so I have to work harder at it?'

She flushed at the compliment, pleased by the idea that she'd made this complex man feel relaxed with her. 'I'll try. And I'm organising tomorrow night. Though I'm afraid my budget won't stretch to anything as fabulous as tonight was. That is, if you want to do something?' Given that he didn't really need to practise his dating skills, it was a bit forward of her to suggest it.

He frowned. 'You don't have to organise anything. The idea is for me to sweep you off your feet.'

'Yes, I do,' she corrected, 'because I'm not a freeloader and I'm going to feel horrible if you pay for everything and sort everything out. And if I feel horrible, then you're not sweeping me off my feet. Quite the opposite.'

'You're stubborn.' To her surprise, he reached out and stroked her face. 'OK. We'll play it your way and you can organise tomorrow night. We agreed to clear our diaries so I won't be working late. I can make any time after seven.'

His touch made her feel all shivery. His eyes went dark and for a moment she thought he was going to dip his head and kiss her. But then he took a step back. 'It's late and we both have work tomorrow. I'd better let you go to bed.'

Grace was relieved and disappointed at the same time. And she couldn't get to sleep for ages, tossing and turning and thinking about the situation. She was horribly aware how easy it would be to fall for Roland Devereux. But this wasn't real, and besides she'd only just come out of a long relationship. She needed to stand on her own two feet for a bit, not just fall for the first man to smile at her.

This was a temporary arrangement. She should just enjoy it for what it was and not be stupid enough to want more.

The next morning, Grace spent her entire journey to work looking up something unusual to do with Roland. Finally she found the perfect thing. She texted him swiftly.

Meet you at seven at Docklands. We're going by Tube. Dress code casual. Do you mind maybe eating a bit late?

It took him a while to reply.

Is fine. What are we doing?

She felt brave enough to text back, Wait and see.

Intrigued, he texted back. Bring it on.

She met him back at the house, but managed to keep him guessing about what they were doing until they were standing in the queue for the pop-up rooftop cinema.

'We're seeing *Back to the Future*?' He smiled. 'Considering what Hugh told me about Bella's first meeting with his family, I should consider myself lucky this isn't *The Sound of Music*.'

'I love that film, but no.' She smiled at him. 'Though you very nearly got *Jaws*.'

He laughed. 'I wouldn't have minded. Actually, I really like the idea of a rooftop cinema.' He eyed the sky. 'Though I hope those are threatening clouds rather than actual rainclouds.'

'They give out ponchos if it's wet,' she said. 'I checked the website.'

He brushed his mouth lightly against hers. 'That doesn't surprise me. You're good at organising things and you pay attention to detail.'

The compliment warmed her all through; and the kiss made her shivery at the knees. She was going to have to be so careful and keep reminding herself that she and Roland weren't really dating. This was simply a practice run for him.

There was a bar selling film-themed cocktails—including a James Bond martini, the White Russian from *The Big Lebowski*, and a Cosmopolitan from *Sex and the City*.

'It's my bill, tonight,' she said firmly. 'Have whatever you like.'

Roland glanced down the list of non-alcoholic cocktails. 'A Shirley Temple for me, please,' he said.

She joined him; they had a brief argument over whether sweet or salted popcorn was better, and ended up sharing a tub of each.

The film was as feel-good and fun as she remembered it. And when Michael J. Fox hitched a ride on his skateboard, she nudged Roland and whispered, 'I can't ever imagine you on a skateboard.'

'No, but I can play the guitar badly enough to make Hugh and Tarq cry—does that count?' he whispered back.

She smiled. 'Just.'

And then the butterflies in her stomach started stampeding as Roland took her hand and laced his fingers through hers. Was this still a practice run? Or did he mean it? He held her hand through the whole film, and she still hadn't worked it out when the first raindrops spattered down.

The ushers swiftly handed out ponchos to the audience, who passed them along the rows of chairs. Grace couldn't help laughing when the ponchos that reached them were pink.

'Hey. I'm comfortable enough with my masculinity to wear pink,' Roland said, and helped her with her poncho before putting on his own.

'Uh-huh.' She was still smiling.

He looked at her. 'What?'

'You, looking all pretty in pink. I should so

grab a picture of that for Hugh and Tarquin,' she said with a grin.

In response he kissed her until she was breathless.

And her concentration was totally shot to pieces.

After the film, they went for a burger. 'I'm afraid this isn't going to be anywhere near up to the standard of last night's food,' Grace said ruefully.

'You're comparing apples and pears,' Roland pointed out, 'and I'm as happy with a burger as I am with gourmet food.'

She scoffed. 'You don't seriously expect me to believe that.'

'I eat out sometimes for work,' he said, 'or when Hugh and Tarq drag me out for our regular catch-up and suggest we go for a curry or a burger. But most of the time for me it's a ready meal at home or a takeaway because I don't really have the time or the inclination to cook.' He looked at her. 'But that meal you cooked me—it was very obvious that you cook on a regular basis.'

'I like cooking,' she said simply. 'It relaxes me.'

'You're really good at it. Did you ever think about going into catering rather than accountancy?'

'You asked me that before.' She shook her head. 'I'm happy with my job—or I will be, if I get offered the one I had the interview for the other day.'

'I'll keep my fingers crossed.' He paused. 'And if you don't get it?'

'Then I'll keep applying until I get a permanent job. But in the meantime the temping tides me over,' she said. 'Anyway, I don't really want to talk about work tonight. Though I guess work is a good topic for a first date when you're trying to get to know someone.'

'As we're sorting out my rusty dating skills, what other topics of conversation would you suggest for a first date?' he asked.

'Things you like and don't like. Say, what kind of films do you normally watch?' She looked at him. 'I'm guessing action movies?'

'Actually, no. I like the old ones that rely on

good direction and acting rather than special effects.'

'Like Hitchcock's films?' she asked. '*Vertigo* and *Rear Window* are two of my favourites.'

'Mine, too,' he said. 'So does this mean you're a film snob at heart?'

She raised an eyebrow. 'Would a film snob go to singalong musical showings?'

He groaned. 'No. Please. Tell me you don't.'

'Oh, I do—that's one thing where Bella and I definitely see things the same way,' she said with a grin. 'You can't beat singing along to *Grease*, *Mamma Mia* or *The Sound of Music* with a cinema full of people.'

'So I really did get off lightly, tonight.'

'You don't like musicals?' she asked.

He grimaced. 'Lyn used to make me watch these terrible rom-coms. I put up with them for her sake, but...' He grimaced again. 'I'm sorry if you think rom-coms are wonderful, too, but they're really not my thing. Musicals aren't quite my thing, either.'

'I'll remember not to drag you along to a rom-com or a musical,' she said. 'Though you're missing out. Doris Day, Gene Kelly—that kind of film is the best thing ever for cheering you up when you've had a bad day.'

'No. That would be going to a gig performed by one of Hugh's pop punk bands,' he corrected. 'Standing right in the middle of the front row, yelling the songs along with them and letting the sound drive everything else out of your head.'

'Pop punk? I'm sure you look great wearing guy-liner,' she teased.

'Oh, please. At thirty, I'm way too old for that.' But he was laughing, and he held her hand all the way to the Tube station—and all the way back to Docklands.

They walked hand in hand along the river frontage in easy silence, watching the play of lights on the water. Grace thought wistfully, if only this was real. But that wasn't the deal, and she needed some space to stand on her own two feet again. So for now she'd just enjoy the moment. Two weeks of being swept off her feet. Wanting more was just greedy.

'I had a really good time tonight,' Roland said.

'Even though it's not the glamorous kind of stuff someone like you is used to?' she asked.

'It was fun,' he said. 'You put a lot of thought into it and came up with something original and different that I really enjoyed. Anyway, it doesn't have to be super-glamorous or cost a lot of money for it to be a good time—like now. There's nothing better than walking by the river at night watching the lights on the water, and that doesn't cost anything.'

'True,' she said. 'I can see why you live here.'

'Is this the sort of area where you'd live, if you had the chance?' he asked.

'Are we talking about my dream home? That would be a pretty little Victorian terraced house, filled with the kind of curtains and cushions you hate most,' she said. 'If I won the lottery, I'd want a place that overlooked somewhere like Hampstead Heath, or have one of those gorgeous houses in Notting Hill that have access to a pretty garden.'

He stopped and turned to face her. 'Like the one in the film where the movie star kisses the ordinary guy?'

'I guess,' she said, and she couldn't help staring at his mouth. Except he wasn't an ordinary guy and she wasn't a film star.

She only realised she'd spoken aloud when he said, 'I'm ordinary enough,' and leaned forward to kiss her.

Time seemed to stop. And she was super-aware of his nearness—his clean male scent, the warmth of his skin, the way the touch of his lips made her skin tingle.

A cat-call from a passing teenager broke the mood, and he took a step back. 'Sorry.'

'It's fine to kiss your date in public,' she said, striving for cool. 'Except maybe not as, um…' How could she tell him that he'd made her feel feverish, without giving herself away? 'A little cooler might be more appropriate,' she said.

'Noted.' But his pupils were huge. Was that because of the darkness around them, or had kissing her affected him the same way it had affected her? She was way too chicken to ask.

And she was even more relieved when her phone pinged. 'This might be my daily Bella-gram,' she said. 'Oh, look—they took a cable car ride today.' She showed him the photograph. 'Trust Bella to hang off the running boards like Doris Day.'

'Wouldn't you do that, too?' he asked.

She gave him a rueful smile. 'I'm the sensible one. I'd be thinking of health and safety.' And missing out on the fun.

'Nothing wrong with being sensible. Do you have plans for tomorrow?' he asked as they headed back to his place.

'No.' Even if they hadn't already agreed to clear their diaries for these next few weeks, she didn't have anything planned.

'You do now—and, no, I'm not telling you what. Dress code is whatever you like. Something comfortable. But bring something warm in case it turns chilly, and I'll bring a golfing umbrella in case it rains.'

They'd be doing something outdoors, then, she guessed. 'What, no pink poncho?' she teased, trying to keep the mood light and not let him guess about how much his kiss had affected her.

'A golfing umbrella is much more appropriate,' he said, unlocking the front door.

'We're playing golf?'

'No—and stop asking questions. It's meant to be spontaneous.'

Spontaneous wasn't how she usually did things. Roland was definitely pushing her out of her comfort zone.

'See you in the morning,' he said. 'And thank you for tonight. I really enjoyed myself.'

'Me, too,' she said.

And although part of her was disappointed that he didn't want to sit with her in his kitchen, drinking coffee and talking about everything under the sun, part of her knew this was the sensible option. She'd nearly lost her head as it was when he'd kissed her. If he kissed her again...

Two weeks, she told herself. She might like the way Roland made her feel, but she was his practice date. This wasn't permanent. Wasn't real. And she'd better remember that.

CHAPTER FIVE

THE NEXT MORNING, Roland was horrified to discover that there was only one firework display set to music in a fifty-mile radius of London—and, worse still, all the tickets to it were already sold.

Oh, for pity's sake.

This was the sort of summer evening event that was often held in the park of a stately home, or possibly in a municipal park or seaside resort as part of a week's carnival event. He couldn't believe that there was only one event available that evening. Surely there had to be others?

He widened the radius for his search, and discovered that the nearest music and fireworks event with a few tickets remaining was being held a hundred miles away. A two-hour drive each end wouldn't be much fun for either of them. So much for sweeping Grace off her feet with something that he actually knew was on her bucket list and she'd really love to do.

Even though he didn't usually use the 'get me a ticket at the last minute' type websites, it looked as if that was going to be his only option. To his relief, he managed to get two tickets for the venue he'd wanted in the first place. That was the hardest bit done, he thought, and headed out to the local deli for part two of his plan. A few minutes later, everything was sorted to his satisfaction.

Roland was sure that this would be the perfect way to sweep Grace off her feet. Even if the weather wasn't on his side and it poured with rain, it wouldn't matter. The fireworks and the music would still go on. And he could set the scene for it, starting right now.

He checked the breakfast tray. Coffee, croissants, freshly squeezed orange juice, granola, Greek yoghurt and a bowl of perfect English strawberries. Philly would forgive him for not buying the sweet peas from her; he'd seen them in a shop window on the way back from the deli and they'd just reminded him of Grace, all sweet and shy. And he hoped that Grace wouldn't mind the fact that the flowers were propped in water in a juice glass rather than in a proper vase.

It was almost nine o'clock. He didn't think that Grace was the sort who'd stay in bed all day; but at the same time she would still have had the chance to relax and sleep in a bit longer than she could on a weekday. Hopefully she wouldn't mind him waking her now. He tucked the newspaper under his arm and carried the tray to her room; he balanced the tray between himself and the wall and knocked on the door. 'Grace?'

'Yes?' Her voice sounded sleepy and he felt a twinge of guilt. Maybe he should've left waking her for another half an hour.

'Can I come in? I've brought you some breakfast.'

'I…sure.'

He walked in to the room. She was sitting in the middle of the king-sized bed, nestled into the duvet, with her hair all mussed and her eyes all sleepy, and his mouth went dry. Oh, help. This wasn't in the plan. He wasn't supposed to react to her like this. He was meant to be sweeping her off her feet, not the other way round. And he definitely needed to keep his eyes off her pretty camisole pyjama top. He absolutely couldn't walk over there, slide the straps from her shoulders and kiss her bare skin. Even though his body was urging him to do exactly that.

'I, um, didn't know what you like for breakfast, but I hoped this would be OK. And I brought you the Saturday paper.'

'Thank you. That's really kind of you. And flowers. That's so lovely.'

Her smile was sweet and shy and genuine, and it made him feel warm inside. 'Pleasure.' He handed her the tray. 'I, um...' How come he was suddenly so flustered and inarticulate? He was known for being as good with words as he was with building, and he could talk anyone through even the most complex project so they understood the plan and loved the concept as much as he did. But, in Grace's presence, all his words seemed to have turned into so much hot air. 'I know we said we'd clear our diaries, but I need to nip into the office and do a few things this morning,' he improvised. 'Would you mind amusing yourself?'

'Roland, you really don't have to entertain me all the time,' she said. 'You're already being kind enough to put me up while the flat's drying out. I don't expect you to run around after me as well.'

'OK.' He couldn't take his eyes off her hair; he wanted to twine the ends round his fingers and see if it was as soft and silky as it looked. So he'd better leave before he did something stupid. 'See you later, then.'

She smiled at him. 'Have a good morning. And thank you for breakfast. This is such a treat. I can't remember the last time someone brought me breakfast in bed.'

Hadn't Howard done that for her? Then again, she'd said they hadn't lived together.

Did that mean they hadn't slept together, either?

That was a question Roland knew he couldn't ask. Not without going into very dangerous territory indeed. Sleeping with Grace… He really had to get that idea out of his head. Fast. Because that wasn't part of the deal he'd made with her. This was about helping her to feel swept off her feet, and helping him to move past the guilt and misery so he could truly live again.

He changed the subject to something safer. 'We need to leave here at about four, if that's OK with you,' he said.

'I'll make sure I'm ready.'

And he knew she'd do exactly that; she prized reliability in others, and that meant in turn that she was always reliable too.

But even when he drove to the office, he found it difficult to concentrate on work instead of thinking about Grace. His foreman, Charlie, who'd come in to the office to debrief him on a project, teased him about being on another planet.

Possibly Planet Crazy, Roland thought, because he just couldn't get Grace Faraday out of his head.

When Roland drove back to London later that afternoon, he had just enough time to drop into the deli to pick up his order and then change into a fresh shirt and a pair of chinos. Grace was ready on time, as he'd expected; her idea of 'smart casual' turned out to be smart black trousers and a pretty strappy top. One which made him remember that pretty camisole top she'd worn in bed that morning, and heat spread through him. 'You look lovely,' he said, meaning it. And somehow he'd have to find that tricky balance between sweeping her off her feet and losing his head completely.

'Thank you,' she said, smiling in acknowledgement of the compliment.

Then he noticed just how sensual the curve of her mouth was. He itched to kiss her, but he managed to hold himself back. Just. 'Ready to go?' he asked, hoping that his voice didn't sound as croaky to her as it did to him.

'Sure.'

He kept the conversation light as he drove Grace to the stately home on the edge of London. Then she saw the banners on the wrought iron fence. 'A classical music and fireworks spectacular? We're actually going to this, right now?'

'You did tell me this sort of thing was on your bucket list,' he pointed out, enjoying the fact that her excitement had sounded in her voice.

'I know, and this is utterly wonderful—but telling you the sort of thing I'd love to do really doesn't mean that I expect you to actually take me to all my dream places,' she said, her face a mixture of delight and guilt.

'But isn't that what you're supposed to do when you sweep someone off their feet? Take them to their dream places?' he asked.

'Maybe.' She bit her lip. 'And that banner says it's sold out.'

'Uh-huh.'

'Don't tell me.' Her voice was dry. 'You called in a favour because you did some work for the people who live here?'

He laughed. 'No. Actually I got our tickets from one of those "get me in at the last minute" sites.'

'What? But they always put a massive mark-up on ticket prices!' She sounded horrified. 'Roland, I need to reimburse you for my ticket.'

He groaned as he followed the car park attendants' direction to a space on the grass. 'Grace, I know you like to be independent, and I appreciate the offer, but you're supposed to be being swept off your feet. Right now, it seems to me that you have both feet very firmly on the ground, so I'm failing miserably.'

She flushed. 'In other words, I'm being an ungrateful brat.'

'No—just a bit difficult,' he said.

'You did tell me that you wanted me to be awkward with you, so you could practise your dating skills on being smooth,' she reminded him.

'Are you telling me you're being difficult on purpose?' His eyes narrowed. 'So how do I know when you're acting and when you're not?'

She spread her hands. 'You tell me.'

He resisted the urge to kiss her until she was breathless—mainly because he knew he'd end up in a similar state, with his head in a spin. Instead, he said, 'Let's go and get set up.' And then maybe the fresh air would help bring him back to his senses. This was meant to be practice dating, not the real thing. She'd made it clear that she didn't want to be let down—and he couldn't trust himself not to repeat his mistakes and let her down.

Roland took a picnic blanket, umbrella, two small collapsible chairs and the wicker picnic hamper from the back of the car.

'What can I carry?' Grace asked.

'Nothing. It's fine.'

'It isn't fine at all. You're totally laden—and there's a big difference between being swept off your feet and being a poor, helpless female who can't carry anything in case she breaks a finger-nail.'

He laughed and she narrowed her eyes at him. 'What's so funny?'

'A week ago, I would've said you were exactly that type.'

'Helpless and pathetic? Well, thank you very much.' She scowled at him.

He winced. 'Grace, I've already told you that I know how much I misjudged you. Though this is particularly bad timing.'

'How do you mean?' she asked.

'Because you're right,' he said. 'I'm fully laden. I'll have to put something down before I can kiss you to say I'm sorry for getting you so wrong.'

'You want to kiss me?'

He moistened his lower lip. 'Firstly to say sorry. And then because...'

Her heart skipped a beat. 'Because what?'

He waited until she met his gaze. 'To say I like you.'

And even though they were outdoors, standing in lush parkland, it felt as if there wasn't enough room to breathe.

'I like you, too,' she whispered. Even though she hadn't expected to. And even though she really didn't want to feel this way about him. She wanted to be independent. She couldn't possibly fall for someone this quickly. Especially someone who'd made a deal with her that he'd sweep her off her feet in exchange for her brushing up his dating skills—because she knew that everything he was saying to her was dating practice, not for real.

'I'm glad you like me,' he said, his voice slightly husky.

Grace knew she ought to leave it there, make him give her a couple of things to carry, and keep it light. But Roland was staring at her mouth, and it was a little too much to resist. She closed the gap between them, stood on tiptoe, and reached up to brush her mouth against his.

When she stepped back, she could see a slash

of vivid colour across his cheeks and his eyes had gone all dark.

'If we weren't in a public place…' His voice cracked.

'But we are,' she said. 'And you need to let me carry something.'

In the end, he let her carry the umbrella and the picnic blanket. They found a nice spot on the lawns with a good view of the stage and the lake—where the fireworks were going to be set off—and between them they spread out the blanket, set up the chairs and opened the picnic basket.

When Grace had gone on picnics as a child, the food had consisted of home-made sandwiches stored in a plastic box, a packet of crisps, an apple and maybe a cupcake or some sausage rolls; there might have been cans of lemonade or cola for her and Bella to drink. Everything had been stored in a cool box, and they'd eaten without plates or cutlery.

This was a whole new level of picnic. Roland's wicker basket had storage compartments for plates, glasses, cutlery, napkins and mugs as well as for the food. And when she helped Roland unpack the food, she discovered that it was on a whole new level from the picnics of her childhood, too. There was artisan seeded bread and butter curls; cold poached chicken with potato salad, watercress and heritage tomatoes; cocktail blinis with cream cheese and smoked salmon; a tub of black olives; oatcakes with crumbly Cheddar, ripe Brie and black grapes; and then strawberries, clotted cream and what looked like very buttery shortbread.

There were bottles of sparkling water, a Thermos which she guessed was filled with coffee, and there was also a tiny bottle of champagne.

'I thought you might like some bubbly to go with your fireworks,' Roland said.

Given what she knew about the tragedy in his past, she felt awkward. 'Are you sure about this?'

He smiled at her. 'I did say I'm fine about other people drinking.'

'Then thank you. This is the perfect size for a treat. Plus it means I won't wake up with a monumental hangover or ask you to make me some banana porridge when we get home,' she said with a smile.

Then she realised what she'd said. *Home.* But the house in Docklands wasn't her home; it was his. She really hoped he hadn't noticed her gaffe.

But he seemed happy enough as he shared the picnic with her.

'So what do women expect to talk about on a date?' he asked.

'I'm probably not the best person to ask, given that I haven't dated that much apart from Howard and…' She let the sentence trail off and grimaced. 'Sorry. I'm not living up to my part of the deal. Let me start again. I guess it's about finding out about each other, and what we've got in common.'

'How do you do that?'

She was pretty sure he already knew that. There was absolutely nothing wrong with his social skills. But she'd go with it for now. 'I guess it's the same as you'd do with any new friendship or even a business relationship—you start with where you are and work from there. If you'd met your date at a swimming pool, you'd ask her how often she came for a swim, or whether she preferred swimming in the pool to swimming in the sea, or where was the nicest place she'd ever been swimming. That sort of thing.'

He smiled. 'So, as we're at a musical event, this is where I ask what sort of music you like? Even though actually I already know that you like popular classical music, and you sing along to the radio.'

She smiled back. 'And then I ask you what you like, even though you already told me yesterday that you like loud pop punk.'

'I do.' He thought about it. 'I like popular classical music as well as indie rock. And I've never been to the opera, but I've been to a few good gigs in my time. Especially since Hugh set up Insurgo.' He paused. 'So that's covered what we listen to. If I extend that to actually playing music—I did about a term's worth of violin lessons before my parents gave in and begged me to stop. What about you?'

'Apart from singing Christmas carols at the infant school nativity play—oh, and playing the triangle for "Twinkle, Twinkle, Little Star" one year and doing it in completely the wrong place—no,' she said. 'None of my friends are musical, either.'

'Some of mine are.' He shrugged. 'But you already know that my best friends own an indie recording label and Hugh's an amazing producer. And your sister gave him his music back. It's great to see him with his heart and soul back in place.'

'I think Hugh and Bella are good for each other,' she said. 'Which reminds me—today's Bellagram.'

Roland burst out laughing when he saw the photograph of Hugh by the railings on Fisherman's Wharf, posing like a sea lion clapping its front feet together, with a crowd of sea lions behind him. 'That's priceless.' He looked at Grace. 'Are you sending her Bellagrams back?'

Grace shook her head. 'If I did, she'd start asking questions—and our deal is just between us.'

'True.' He paused. 'OK. That's music done. What next? I know you can cook, and you know I don't bother. We both like good food.'

'And, even though you might not cook something yourself, you make great choices. This cheese is amazing,' she said, helping herself to another slice of the Cheddar with an oatcake.

'Food, music. Next topic.' He looked thoughtful. 'Travel?'

'I haven't travelled that much,' she admitted.

Because she was scared of flying? Or had she just never had the chance to travel?

If it was the latter, Roland thought, this was a definite sweeping-off-feet opportunity. The perfect way to end their time together, even. He knew exactly where he was going to take her. He'd book it later tonight.

'Do you have a passport?' he checked.

She nodded.

Good, he thought. That was the biggest barrier out of the way. Then he remembered that she'd called off her wedding very recently and grimaced. 'Sorry. Did I just put my foot in it? Had you booked an amazing honeymoon in Hawaii or something?'

She shook her head. 'Howard wasn't really one for long-haul flights—or even short-haul, really. We were going to drive down to the south of France. Cynthia had asked a couple of her friends to lend us their flat.'

Who on earth organised their son's honeymoon, unless it was a special surprise and something that the happy couple couldn't afford to do for themselves? Roland wondered. And although a borrowed flat in the South of France would be very nice for a short break, he didn't understand why a qualified accountant who worked for the family firm—and therefore had to be on a pretty decent salary—couldn't afford to book something a little more special for his honeymoon. So either Howard and his family were very mean with money, or his mother was a control freak who refused to let her son make his own decisions. Either way, it sounded as if Grace had had a lucky escape.

'The South of France is nice,' he said carefully.

'But not where you'd choose for a honeymoon?' she asked, picking up on his hesitation.

'No,' he admitted. 'And definitely not a borrowed flat if I could afford to pay for somewhere myself.'

'Where did you and Lynette go?' she asked.

Then she bit her lip. 'Sorry. That was nosey. I didn't mean to bring up memories.'

'They're good memories,' he said. And, surprisingly, it didn't hurt to talk about Lynette to Grace. It was actually nice to remember the times when they'd been happy. Before the baby-making project had put so much pressure on them both and their marriage had started to crack under the strain. 'We went to the rainforest in Brazil and stayed in a treetop hotel.'

'That sounds amazing,' she said wistfully.

'It was a kind of private oasis,' he said. 'We could sit out on the balcony and watch the monkeys and hear the macaws. There were wooden catwalks through the canopy of trees, so walking between our suite and the dining room was amazing. There was even a treetop swimming pool.'

'That's really exotic,' she said.

'I've never been anywhere like it—swimming with all these tropical birds flying just over your heads. And the food was great; every night we had fresh grilled fish, beans and rice and amazing bread, and exotic fruit. The day I remember most was when we took a boat trip on the Amazon and swam with the pink freshwater dolphins.'

'That sounds perfect,' Grace said wistfully.

'It was the trip of a lifetime,' he said. 'We'd both always wanted to see the rainforest, and it more than lived up to our expectations. I'm not sure whether I liked the sunrise or the sunset most, or just looking up into the sky and seeing a different set of stars, so bright against the darkness of the sky and so very different from London.' He paused. 'So what about you? What's your dream trip?' The one that her ex-fiancé hadn't made come true.

'It's a bit nerdy.'

He smiled. He'd expect nothing less from Grace. 'Nerdy's good. Tell me.'

'I'd love to go on the Orient Express,' she said, 'all the way from Paris to Istanbul.' She shrugged. 'But that particular trip is only scheduled once a year.'

If Roland had been planning to get married to Grace, he would've arranged their wedding so they could start their honeymoon with the train journey from Paris to Istanbul before venturing further afield. Why hadn't Howard done that? Didn't he like trains? Or had he never bothered to find out what made his fiancée tick?

Not that it was any of Roland's business. And he wasn't planning to get married any time soon. This was practice dating, he reminded himself. Talking to his date and finding out more about her. 'Where else would you like to go?'

'Do you mean my fantasy travel wish-list—the really wild stuff that I know I'm never actually going to do?' she asked. At his nod, she continued, 'I'd like to go to Australia and see the stars in the outback, and to Alaska to see the glaciers and the whales, and maybe the Antarctic to see the penguins, and to walk along some of the Great Wall of China.' She paused. 'How about you?'

'Actually, I like the sound of all of those.' He was faintly shocked by how much their tastes dovetailed. Only a few days ago, he would've said that they had nothing in common. But it looked as if some of her dreams were very similar to his own.

'You haven't already done them?' She looked surprised.

'No. Lyn really liked city breaks, so I've been to all the big cities in Europe,' he explained, 'plus New York, Boston, San Francisco and LA. And I've travelled pretty extensively on business, with conferences and the like; I always try to spend a day looking round wherever I'm based.'

'So where would you go for your fantasy travel list?' she asked.

'I'd like to see the Victoria Falls, and swim in the Blue Lagoon in Iceland,' he said. 'And visit Yosemite, to see the hot springs and waterfalls.'

'So it's water that draws you?'

'I've never thought about it that way, but yes, I suppose it is,' he said, surprised. 'Venice is one of my favourite places ever, and I love the sea. There's nothing better than walking on the cliffs with the waves crashing below and sending spray everywhere. Or strolling on a flat sandy beach in the moonlight with the sea all calm and just lapping at the shore.'

'Plus you live right on the Thames,' she pointed out.

'And you could never keep me off the lake as a boy.'

'Would this lake be at one of the chateaux?' she asked.

'No. At my family home in Kent,' he admitted.

'You had a lake?' She blinked. 'So are you telling me that you grew up somewhere like this?' She gestured to the stately home in front of them.

He squirmed. This felt like bragging—and that wasn't who he was. 'It's not as big as this. But, um…yes, I guess it's this sort of thing. Though it's been in the family for generations, and the roof is a total money pit, to the point where Dad's opened the gardens to the public, and we're turning the boathouse at the lake into a café.'

'And would I be right in guessing that his favourite architect,' she asked with a grin, 'is going to suggest having a glass wall all along the side of the building that faces the lake?'

'You are.' He smiled back at her. 'Though I guess that was obvious.'

'Not necessarily. Do you have another brother or sister who's an architect?'

He shook his head. 'Will's the oldest, so he's

pretty much involved with the estate because he'll take over from Dad. Actually, he's already doing his own projects—he's sorting out a licence so we can hold wedding ceremonies. I'm the middle child, and I get hauled in to look at the roof from time to time and give my professional opinion on any renovation work that crops up. And Philly's the baby—she basically adopted the head gardener as her honorary uncle when she was a toddler and moved up to nagging him to let her have a corner of the greenhouse all to herself by the time she was ten. So it was always obvious that she'd end up being either a landscape gardener or a florist. And she's brilliant. Really gifted.'

'You sound close to your family,' she said.

'I am.' He smiled. 'And you're close to yours.'

'I'm lucky,' she said simply.

He could tell that Grace was thinking about her almost-in-laws. What he didn't understand was why on earth her ex-fiancé's family hadn't liked her. She was sensible, kind and tactful. And, once you got past her shyness, she was fun. Yes, she had a nerdy streak, but that meant she looked at things from a different viewpoint—and in turn that made him look at things differently, too.

Though this dating thing was a temporary deal. And she'd just come out of a long relationship; she'd made it clear that she didn't want to rush into anything new. He didn't want to rush into anything, either. So he needed to keep these burgeoning feelings firmly under control, because they just weren't appropriate.

The orchestra began playing on stage, so he was saved from further conversation. But every so often he sneaked a glance at Grace to check that she was enjoying herself. And once or twice he caught her sneaking a glance at him, too. In the darkening evening, her cornflower-blue eyes were almost navy. Hypnotic.

As the fireworks began, he found himself sliding an arm across the back of her chair. If she asked, he'd say it was because he was worried she might be cold—English summer evenings weren't that warm. He certainly wouldn't tell her that it was because he wanted to be close to her. 'OK?' he asked.

'Very OK,' she said with a smile. 'This is absolutely gorgeous—the music, the fireworks and the reflections. It's the perfect combination. Thank you so much for bringing me.'

'My pleasure,' he said, meaning it. He couldn't remember when he'd relaxed so much, just enjoying his surroundings and chilling out. And he knew it was all down to Grace. Her quiet calmness made him feel grounded.

Maybe, he thought, he should suggest turning this from a practice run to a real relationship. See where it took them. But would she say yes? Or would she back away?

He managed to keep his thoughts under control during the fireworks, and driving home in the dark meant that he needed to concentrate and didn't have the headspace for thinking. But once they were back in Docklands he found the question buzzing through his head again.

Should he ask her?

Or should he do the sensible thing and back away?

In the end, Grace made the decision for him, by kissing him on the cheek. 'Thank you for tonight, Roland. It was every bit as fabulous as I dreamed it would be. And it was even nicer because it was a total surprise.'

'My pleasure,' he said automatically. She'd kissed his cheek, not his mouth. Meaning that he needed to back off.

Before he could suggest making a drink so he could linger in her company just that little bit longer, she said, 'I'll see you in the morning, then. Good night.'

'Good night,' he said. 'Sleep well.'

Though he had a feeling that he wouldn't. Grace was stirring feelings in him that he thought were long buried. And, even though he was usually so sure about what he was doing, right now he felt as if he was walking blindfold along a path littered with lumps and bumps and holes, having to feel his way to make sure he stayed on his feet.

Maybe he'd manage to get his common sense back into place overnight.

Maybe.

CHAPTER SIX

GRACE'S MOUTH WAS soft and sweet, and Roland couldn't get enough of it. Yet he wanted a deeper intimacy, too. He'd just unzipped her dress when he heard something banging.

Then he realised it was the door.

His bedroom door.

And he was completely alone in bed. It was Sunday morning, and he'd been dreaming about making love with Grace. Heat rushed through his cheeks.

'Roland? Can I come in?' a voice called.

Grace.

The heat in his face intensified. No way did he want her to have any idea what he'd just been thinking about. On the other hand, he didn't have a valid excuse to tell her to go away. 'Uh—yeah,' he mumbled, hoping that he'd be able to think on his feet, and sat up.

She walked in carrying a tray. 'No sweet peas, I'm afraid. But I hope you'll like this.' Then she looked at his bare chest and blushed. 'Um. Sorry. I didn't realise...'

'I'm wearing pyjama bottoms,' he said hastily. But he was very glad that the duvet was piled in his lap and hid his arousal. He didn't want to embarrass either of them.

When she handed him the tray, he realised that she'd brought him coffee and Eggs Benedict. It looked and smelled amazing.

'Is that home-made Hollandaise sauce?' he asked.

'Yes.'

'If you ever get tired of working with numbers,' he said, 'I guarantee you'd have a fantastic career if you opened your own restaurant.' He still didn't get why she wasn't using her talent. Why she was hiding behind numbers.

'I like cooking for fun,' she said. 'Cooking as a business would be a totally different ballgame. And it'd be sad if something I really enjoy doing turned out to be something I felt I was forced to do. Not to mention the unsociable hours I'd need to work; I wouldn't get to see enough of my parents and Bella.'

'I guess,' he said. And it was a logical explanation, one he couldn't argue with.

'It's my turn to organise things today,' she said. 'That is, if you'd like to do something with me and you don't have to work?'

Maybe he should grab this opportunity to put a little distance between them.

Except his mouth wasn't working from the same script as his head and using his usual cast-iron excuse of working on some architectural design or other, because he found himself saying, 'I'd like to do something with you.'

'Great. Maybe we can be ready to leave in an hour?' she suggested.

'I can be ready before that. What are we doing?'

'Something immensely nerdy, but I hope you'll enjoy it,' she said with a smile. 'See you later.'

He watched her walk out of the room, noting the sway of her hips. He was definitely going to need a cold shower after breakfast. And it had been a while since he'd had such a graphic dream.

So did that mean that he was ready to start to move on?

With Grace?

But she'd only just come out of a long relationship where she hadn't been happy. And although she'd said that she'd wanted to be swept off her feet, the Grace he was beginning to get to know liked structure and organisation. She was very far from being the sort to rush into things. He needed to be careful with her.

Which meant not giving in to the urge to sweep her off her feet, literally, and carrying her to his bed.

The cold shower was enough to restore some of his common sense. He shaved, got dressed, and found her in the kitchen doing a number puzzle in a magazine.

He smiled. 'Would this be your Sunday morning guilty pleasure?'

'Busted,' she said ruefully.

He glanced over her shoulder at the page. 'That doesn't look like the kind of thing you see in the newspaper supplements.'

'I suppose it's for people who like, um, really

nerdy puzzles. My parents buy me a subscription to this magazine every Christmas,' she admitted.

'Don't hide your light under a bushel,' he said. 'Most people couldn't do these sorts of puzzles. Be proud of yourself because you can.' And why was she so diffident about her abilities? That was really bugging him. He'd actually met her family and liked them. They weren't the sort who'd do someone down to boost their own ego. So who had made Grace feel bad about herself and hide who she was? 'Would I be right in guessing that your ex didn't like you doing them?'

'No.'

But she looked away, and he guessed that yet again her ex's disapproving mother had been the sticking point.

'Not everyone likes puzzles,' she said, still not meeting his eye.

'Which doesn't mean you should take away the fun from those who do.' And it made him wonder why Grace's ex had put up with the situation. If his own mother had been difficult with Lyn, he would've taken his mother to one side and gently explained that he'd made his life choice and he'd prefer her to respect that and treat his partner with a bit more courtesy—even if they couldn't be close friends, they could still be civil to each other. Though Roland's mother wasn't the cold, judgemental type who placed importance upon appearances above all else, and he knew that his whole family would adore Grace. She would adore them, too.

Not that he intended to introduce them to each other. This was way, way too soon.

She closed her magazine. 'I'll just do the washing u—' she began.

'No,' Roland said, and put everything from his tray in the dishwasher before she could argue. 'Didn't you say you wanted to leave soon?'

'Yes. And it's my trip, so we're going in my car.'

'Yes, ma'am,' he teased.

As he'd expected, Grace turned out to be a very competent driver, but he didn't have a clue where they were going until she turned off at Bletchley Park. 'I should've guessed you'd plan to visit somewhere like this,' he said.

'Why?'

The expression on her face was fleeting, but he'd noticed it. Expecting that she'd be judged—and judged harshly. Although Roland didn't believe that violence solved anything, he would've liked to shake Howard's mother until her teeth rattled. Grace had been engaged to Howard for four years, so they'd probably dated for a year or so before then—meaning that the woman had had five years to crush Grace's confidence. And how. The fact that Grace had still had the guts to walk away from the situation was a testimony to her strength. 'You like numbers, so this place must be fascinating for you,' he said. 'If you'd been alive in those times, I think they would've asked you to work here, given that you're good at puzzles.'

'And if you'd been alive in those times, you might've been working on the architecture for the Mulberry harbour or something like that,' she said.

'Or working with the guy who was trying to find an alternative material to build the Mosquito planes when there was a shortage of balsa wood,' he said thoughtfully. 'There was a chemist who was working on making a foam from seaweed that dried into planks that would be as strong as wood.'

She glanced at him. 'A plane made from seaweed? I assume you're teasing me?'

'No, I'm serious,' he said. 'I read an article about it in a professional journal. Apparently one of the seaweed "planks" is in the Science Museum in London.'

'What an amazing story,' she said. 'I'm going to have to go to the Science Museum now to see it for myself.'

'Maybe we can go together.' The words were out before he could stop them. This was dangerous. He wasn't supposed to be finding shared points of interest for the future. They'd agreed to help each other out, not fall for each other.

'Maybe we can go next weekend, or on one of the evenings when they open late.' She gave him another of those shy smiles, then parked the car. 'We don't need to queue, by the way. I bought tickets online while you were in the shower this morning, and I've already downloaded the multimedia guide to my phone,' she said.

Typical Grace, being organised and thorough. 'Sounds good.' He took her hand and they wandered round, enjoying the sunshine and exploring the different code-breaking huts.

'I love the way they've done this so you can actually feel what it was like to work here—even down to the sounds and smells,' he said.

'Me, too,' she said. 'I hoped you'd like this— you said you liked museums and buildings, and this is... Well.'

'It's brilliant. And I'm going to be totally boring when we get to the displays about how they restored the buildings.' He kissed her to reassure her that he was happy with her choice of date, but kept it swift so he could keep his feelings in control.

They lingered in the display about the Enigma machines, and the Bombe machine that finally cracked the code. He could see how interested she was, and how her eyes lit up. If he was honest with himself, she fascinated him as much as this place fascinated her. He hadn't met anyone quite like her before. Lyn had been outgoing and confident—at least, until the baby-making plan had gone wrong—and Grace was quiet and shy and kept a lot of herself hidden. Yet something about her drew him. He wanted to take down all her barriers and let her shine.

They stopped for lunch in the site's café. 'So when did you know you wanted to work with numbers?' he asked.

She shrugged. 'I just always liked numbers. Dad found me trying to do the number puzzles in the Sunday supplements, so he started buying me puzzle magazines. My favourite ones were where you have to fit a list of numbers instead of words into a grid. Then I moved up to logic puzzles and Sudoku. I, um, won a competition at school for being the fastest at solving them,' she added shyly.

'And you never thought about going to university to study maths?'

'One of my teachers tried to get me to apply to

Oxford,' she said, 'but I don't think I was cut out to be a teacher. It seemed a bit pointless spending three years studying and getting into debt when I could've been learning on the job and making progress in my professional exams.'

Sensible and measured and reliable: that was Grace. Though he wondered what would've happened if she'd let herself have the chance to work with the more abstract branches of mathematics—how far she would've soared.

'And that's where you met Howard, when you were training?'

She shook her head. 'I qualified in a different firm, then moved to Sutton's because there was an opportunity for promotion. I never expected to fall for the boss's son, but we worked together on an audit when I'd been there for six months and he asked me out.'

Roland had the feeling that Grace had concentrated on her studies rather than on partying. He wouldn't be surprised if Howard had been her first serious boyfriend.

'And you liked him?' he asked.

She nodded. 'He was sweet and kind—and I

guess I was a bit naive because I thought that his parents would eventually warm to me. I'm not a gold-digger.'

'Of course you're not,' he said. But clearly Howard's parents had treated her as if she was. It made Roland understand where her insistence on being independent and doing her fair share came from. Clearly she'd had to prove herself over and over and over again. But why hadn't her ex stood up for her? And why had it taken her so long to realise that she was worth more than the way his family treated her?

'How about you?' she asked. 'How did you meet Lynette?'

'We worked together,' he said. 'I was an architect and she was a PA at the practice. We danced together at an office Christmas party, and that was it.'

'So you knew straight away that she was The One?'

'I guess.' He nodded. 'We moved in together fairly quickly, but she insisted on a long engagement when I asked her to marry me.'

'But not four years?' Grace asked wryly.

Roland smiled. 'Just one. And that was long enough. Though I guess she was right; it gave us time to get to know each other properly and be really sure we were doing the right thing. And we were happy.' Until that last year of their marriage, when Lyn's friends all seemed to fall pregnant the very first month they started trying, while he had to comfort his wife every month when her period arrived. The doctors had all said they were young and it was too early to think about fertility treatment, and advised them both just to relax and keep trying; but sex in those last six months had been all about making a baby and not at all about expressing their love for each other. Lyn had charts and ovulation kits every-where, and every time they'd made love it had been carefully timed rather than simply because they wanted each other.

Roland had started taking every opportunity to work away, or to give a paper at a confer-ence, just to take the pressure off and make him feel less like a machine. And that was why he'd bought the house at the maltings—something that would take over his head completely. Something he could escape to.

Not that he'd told anyone about it. Not his family and not his closest friends. How could he tell them that he'd felt a failure as a husband, that he'd let Lyn down every single month?

And the cruellest irony of all had been when the doctor at the hospital had told him...

He dragged in a breath. Not now. He wasn't going to think of that now.

She laid her hand against his cheek. 'I'm sorry, Roland. I didn't mean to bring back bad memories for you.'

Yeah. They must've shown on his face. But he didn't have the words to tell anyone about the worst bit. He hadn't even told Lyn's parents. Which made him a seriously bad person, because he really shouldn't have kept it from them. Or maybe it had been kinder not to tell them. 'It's OK. But I could do with changing the subject,' he admitted. He still found it hard to handle the guilt. Although he knew it wasn't his fault that the drunken driver had crashed into Lyn's car, and it was entirely possible that the crash could've happened even if he'd been at home, he still couldn't forgive himself for not being there at the end— or handle that last, unkindest cut of all.

'Let's go and look round a bit more,' she said.

And funny how comforting he found it when her hand curled round his as they walked round the site. She didn't push him to talk; she was just there, offering quiet support and kindness.

If he wanted to make this thing between them real, he'd have to tell her the truth. All of it. Including the stuff he didn't let himself think about. He didn't think she'd pity him, and she definitely wouldn't judge him. But he still wasn't ready to talk, and he wasn't sure if he ever would be. Maybe brushing up his dating skills was a bad idea. Or maybe he'd work out some way to move things forward between them without opening up that world of hurt.

On Monday morning, Grace picked up a text from Roland during her break.

Can you get Wednesday to Friday off this week?

Why? she texted back.

Sweeping-off-feet stuff was the response. Which told her nothing.

I'll see what I can do, she said.

Possibly because it was still June, before the summer holiday season started in earnest, the office where she was working was happy for her to take the time off.

'Excellent,' Roland said when she told him the news.

She coughed. '"Sweeping-off-feet stuff" is all very well, but if we're going away somewhere I need to know what to pack.'

'A couple of nice dresses and something for walking about in,' he said.

'Walking about—do you mean walking boots, waterproofs and insect repellent?' she asked.

'Nope. Smart casual.'

'So it's urban and not country, then?'

He sighed. 'Grace, I can hardly sweep you off your feet if you know all the details.'

'But if I don't know enough, I'll need three suitcases so I can be prepared for every eventuality,' she countered.

He smiled. 'Minimal luggage would be better. OK. It's urban. I'm not planning to make you walk along most of Hadrian's Wall—though,' he added, 'if you're up for that...'

Grace pushed away the thought that she'd go anywhere with him. Because this thing between them wasn't permanent. 'Uh-huh,' she said, hoping that she sounded polite enough but not committing herself to anything. 'Got it. Minimal luggage, a couple of smart dresses, and smart casual stuff with shoes I can walk in.' Quite what he had in mind, she had no idea.

'And your passport,' he said.

'My passport? Bu—'

He silenced her protest by the simple act of kissing her. 'It's sweeping-off-feet stuff,' he reminded her gently. 'And my bank balance can definitely take it, before you start protesting or feeling guilty. It's a place I'd like to show you, so please just give in...' He laughed. 'I would say gracefully, but, given your name, doing something "Gracefully" means asserting your independence and being stroppy.'

She nodded, simply because that kiss had wiped

out anything she'd intended to say. And he just smiled and kissed her again. 'Sweeping you off your feet. That was the deal,' he said.

And how.

CHAPTER SEVEN

'REMIND ME NEVER to play poker with you,' Grace grumbled as they got on the Tube. 'You have to be the most...' She shook her head, unable to think of the words.

'Poker-faced?' Roland teased.

'Annoying,' she retorted.

Roland just laughed. 'If I told you where we were going, then I wouldn't be sweeping you off your feet. Trust me. It'll be worth it.'

Grace wasn't so sure—until he led her to a platform at Victoria station and she realised what was standing in front of them. An old-fashioned train, with the staff all lined up in front of it, wearing posh livery.

'This is the London starting point of the Orient Express.' She caught her breath. He couldn't mean this—could he? 'We're going on this? Now? Really?'

He looked utterly pleased with himself. 'Yup. I was paying attention when we talked at the fireworks, you know.'

And how. This was something she'd dreamed about doing for years and years, and never thought she'd ever actually do. When she'd mentioned it to Howard, he'd clearly discussed it with his mother because he'd told her the next day that it was way too extravagant and there were much better, cheaper and more efficient ways of going to Paris than the Orient Express.

Not that she'd ever been to Paris. Since she'd been dating Howard, they'd always been too busy at work to take off more than a couple of days at a time, which they usually spent in a cottage somewhere in England—even though Paris was only two hours away from London on the Eurostar.

And now Roland was taking her on her dream trip. Although they weren't going all the way to Istanbul—because that particular journey was only scheduled for once a year, and even Roland couldn't change that—they were still taking a slow train to Paris, the City of Light. The most romantic place in Europe.

He was really sweeping her off her feet.

She realised that he was waiting for her to say something, but right now she was so overwhelmed that she couldn't think straight, let alone string a proper sentence together. 'Roland, I don't know what to say.'

'"Thank you, Roland, it's nice to tick something off my bucket list" would do,' he teased.

'It is, and it's fabulous, and I'm stunned because I never expected you to do anything like this, but—'

As if he guessed she was about to protest about the cost, he cut off her words by kissing her.

'Grace, I wouldn't have booked this if I couldn't afford it,' he said, 'and I'm actually quite enjoying sweeping you off your feet. Do you have any idea how good it makes me feel, knowing that I'm able to make one of your dreams come true?'

It was something she knew she'd like to do for him, too. Except Roland hadn't really shared his dreams with her, so she had no idea what she could do to make him feel this same surge of delight. She took a deep breath. 'OK. Brattish protesting about the cost all swept to one side. This is really fantastic and I'm utterly thrilled. I can't believe you've done something so amazing and lovely for me, but I'm really glad you have.' And she meant that, from the bottom of her heart. 'Thank you so much. This is the best treat ever.'

'I'm glad you're enjoying it.' He took her hand. 'Let me escort you to our seat, *mademoiselle*.'

Roland had said that there was a French branch of his family, and given that his surname sounded French she could entirely believe it; but this was the first time she'd ever heard him speak the language. Admittedly, it was only one word, but it was amazing how much sexier he sounded in French.

And then she made the mistake of telling him that.

He grinned and launched into a rapid stream of French.

She coughed. 'My French is limited to school-girl stuff, and that's pretty rusty. I understood maybe one word in ten out of that. Even if you said it all again at half the speed, I still wouldn't understand much more.'

'Maybe,' he said, 'I'll show you later instead.'

And, oh, the pictures that put in her head. Heat rushed through her and her face felt as if it had turned a vivid shade of beetroot.

He simply gave her the most wicked and sultry smile.

Not only was Grace feeling swept off her feet, she was in severe danger of losing her head as well. And, even though she was loving every second of this, part of her felt way out of her depth. So she'd just have to remind herself that she was sensible and this was two weeks of sheer fun— he didn't expect her to fit into this environment permanently.

When they got to their carriage, it was nothing like the trains she normally used outside London. There was plenty of space, and the plush, comfortable seats were placed opposite each other in pairs, with the small table in between covered by a white damask cloth.

'I forgot to ask if you get travel sick,' Roland said, suddenly looking horrified. 'Sorry. Would you prefer to face the direction we're travelling?'

'I don't get sick, exactly,' she said, 'but yes, please—if that's OK with you?'

'Of course it is.'

But the luxury didn't stop at their seats. The waiter came to serve them their drinks—freshly squeezed orange juice for Roland, and a Bellini for Grace.

'This is so decadent,' Grace said with delight, giving herself up to the pleasure of being pampered.

Brunch was even nicer—fresh fruit salad, followed by crumpets with smoked salmon, caviar and scrambled eggs, then pastries and coffee. And everything was slow and unhurried, as if they had all the time in the world. So very different from the usual rush of a working life in London.

At Folkestone, they were met by a band serenading them, and then took the bus through the Eurotunnel to Calais. At the station, they were met by another band playing; and on the platform where the vintage blue and gold train was waiting, the staff were lined up in their smart blue uniforms and peaked hats. The restaurant staff were clad in white jackets with gold braid, black trousers and white gloves.

'I feel like a princess,' Grace whispered.

'Good. That's the idea.' Roland squeezed her hand. 'Now for the real thing,' he said with a smile. 'The Orient Express over mainland Europe.'

One of the uniformed staff took them to their cabin; it was cosy yet beautifully presented, and Grace had never seen anything so luxurious in her life.

Again, the pace was slow and unhurried. If they'd taken the express train from St Pancras, they would've been in Paris already; but the slow journey through the French countryside was so much nicer, giving them time to look at their surroundings.

'So tell me about the French side of your family,' she said. 'Didn't you say they have vineyards?'

He nodded. 'They're all in the Burgundy area. One branch of the family produces Chablis, and the other produces Côtes de Nuits.' He grinned. 'They're horribly competitive—but luckily because one specialises in white wine and one specialises in red, they're not in competition with each other. But there's a kind of race every year about how many awards and glowing reviews they can get.'

'But I bet they're the only ones allowed to be rude about each other, right?'

His eyes glittered with amusement. 'Right.'

'So do you see them very often?'

'Not as often as I'd like,' he admitted. 'It's very pretty in Dijon, with all the old narrow streets and houses built of honey-coloured stone. The whole area is lovely and the views from the chateaux are amazing. Actually, I really ought to go and visit them soon, because I've been getting pleading emails about difficult roofs and I did promise to go and have a look.'

'Do all old buildings have problematic roofs?' she asked, remembering what he'd said about the roof in his family home.

'It's not just that—there's damp, dry rot, death watch beetle, subsidence...' He spread his hands. 'And if someone hasn't been careful enough to use the right materials when working on an old house—using modern plaster instead of lime, for example, or replacing a wooden floor with concrete—it can create more problems than it solves.' He smiled. 'But I'm not going to drone on about restoration work.'

'Or glass?' she teased.

'There's one glass building I'm definitely taking you to see in Paris,' he said. 'But don't ask me what. It's a surprise.'

'No asking. I promise,' she said.

'One thing I was wondering about you, though,' he said. 'Why do you worry about the cost of things so much?'

She grimaced. 'This stays with you? You're not going to say a word to Bella?'

'It stays with me,' he promised.

'I guess it stems from when I was little,' she said. 'My father wasn't just unreliable about time—he wasn't very good with money, either. I can remember the bailiffs coming round when I was about three, and it was pretty scary. I remember my mum crying her heart out when she thought I was asleep. I don't ever want to be in that situation again.' She shrugged. 'Which is why I'm always very careful with money. I'm being sensible.'

'I wasn't accusing you of being a Scrooge,' he said swiftly. 'But don't you ever feel you've missed out, sometimes?'

'No.' But her denial was too swift, and she could see in his expression that he thought so, too. And, yes, she knew she'd missed out on things in the past because she'd been too sensible and too careful. Just as she would've missed out on this trip today if she hadn't for once thrown caution to the wind and agreed to his suggestion of helping each other out. 'Can we change the subject?' she asked, feeling antsy and cross with herself because she was ruining the mood.

'Sure.'

'Tell me about Paris,' she said. 'The first time you went there and what you really loved.'

'That's easy,' he said. 'My parents took all three of us, on the way down to Bordeaux. I must've been about five. It was Christmas, and we went to the Galeries Lafayette. The Christmas tree there was the tallest one I've ever seen in my life—before or since—and it was covered in lights and shiny red apples. And we went to a café for hot chocolate that had a cinnamon stick in it—something I'd never really seen in England—and we all had a slice of chocolate cake from the *bûche de Noël*. And my mum bought poinsettias.' He smiled. 'Philly of course loved the fact they're called *étoile de Noël* because the leaves are star-shaped and red, gold and green are the colours of Christmas in France. She always does them up the French way in her shop at Christmas.'

Grace relaxed again as Roland chatted easily with her about Paris and Christmas and how his family mixed both French and English traditions.

'It's nice to include both bits of your heritage, though—the English and the French.'

'Yes, it is,' he agreed.

They dressed up for an early dinner in the dining car—Grace was really glad she'd bought a new cocktail dress during her lunch break the previous day—and every course was sumptuous and exquisitely presented, from the lobster to the tournedos Rossini, the platter of French cheeses, and then a cone of coconut sorbet with a delicate slice of fresh pineapple that had been caramelised.

'This is beyond what I dreamed it would be

like on the Orient Express,' she said to Roland when their coffee arrived. 'Thank you so much.'

'Je t'en prie,' he said.

'Um—I don't remember what that means.'

'You're welcome,' he said. 'And we haven't reached Paris yet. I hope you'll like what I've planned.'

'If it's even one per cent as fabulous as this,' she said, 'I'll love it.'

Roland had arranged for a plush car to meet them at the station and take them to the centre of the city. Grace drank in their surroundings in total silence as they drove through the centre of Paris, not wanting to break the spell; she'd had no idea just how pretty the city was. The wide boulevards, the pretty buildings, the light and airy feel of the place.

The outside of their hotel was beautiful, a five-storey white building with long narrow windows and wrought iron balconies—just what she'd imagined a Parisian hotel to look like. Inside, it was even better: the lobby was all white walls with gilt-framed pictures, red and white marble chequered flooring and wrought iron chandeliers. At the end was a marble staircase with a wrought iron and gilded balustrade. She'd never seen anything so glittering and gorgeous.

When the concierge took them up to their floor, her pulse speeded up. So this was it. Sharing a room with Roland.

As if he'd guessed her sudden nervousness, he said, 'We have a suite. There are two bedrooms and two bathrooms. I'm not taking anything for granted.'

So he wasn't expecting her to sleep with him. 'Thank you,' she said.

But, even though they hadn't known each other for very long and they weren't in a permanent relationship—and weren't planning to be in one, either—Grace knew that if he asked her to make love with him while they were in Paris, her answer would be yes. How could she resist him in the most romantic city in the world?

Her bedroom was gorgeous, with a pale blue carpet, cream walls, and tall windows that opened onto a balcony with an amazing view of the Eiffel Tower. Her bed was wide, with plenty of deep, fluffy pillows; and the bathroom was all cream marble and gilding. When she came back into the living room between the bedrooms, she noticed that there were comfortable chairs and sofas upholstered in old gold, and there was a vase of fresh flowers on the coffee table.

'This is amazing, Roland,' she said.

He smiled. 'Yes, it's pretty good.'

Had he stayed here before? Did this bring back memories of his late wife? But she didn't want to hurt him by asking.

He didn't seem to notice her awkwardness, because he said, 'And now we have an evening in Paris.'

An evening in Paris. It sounded incredibly romantic. And he said he'd planned things. 'What do you have in mind?' she asked.

'Come with me,' he said.

He'd retained the plush car from before. 'It would take us an hour to walk where I'm taking you, and the Métro journey means a lot of messing about, so that's why we're taking a car now,' he explained. 'We can walk through the city and explore tomorrow.'

'OK,' she said.

They ended up at what he told her was the fifth *arrondissement*. 'This is Quai St Bernard,' he said, 'and it's the perfect place for a summer evening.'

There was a mini amphitheatre on the side of the Seine. People were sitting on the side of the river, picnicking or drinking wine and listening to the DJ playing what sounded like tango music; and there was a crowd of people dancing.

'Tangoing in Paris?' she asked. 'Roland—this is fabulous, but I'm afraid I don't know how to tango. Though I'm very happy to watch the dancing,' she added swiftly, not wanting him to think she was ungrateful. 'I can still soak up the atmosphere and enjoy it.'

'I know you do dance aerobics with Bella, so you can follow a routine,' he said. 'Don't worry that you've never danced a tango before. You'll pick it up. Just follow my lead.'

And what could she do but give in to the steady, hypnotic beat and dance with him? He held her really close, sliding one thigh between hers and spinning her round, and it was his nearness rather than the dancing that took her breath away.

When he bent her back over his arm, his mouth skimmed the curve of her throat and she went hot all over. If there hadn't been so many strangers dancing around them—if he'd danced with her like this in the privacy of their hotel suite—she knew this would've been the prelude to a much deeper intimacy. She could see from the expression in Roland's dark eyes that right now he felt exactly the same way. And although part of her felt shy about it, part of her revelled in it. In being totally swept off her feet, dancing the tango by the river in Paris at night.

The music changed to a salsa—something she did know, from her aerobics classes—and Roland smiled as she segued into the step-ball-change routine, side to side and back to front.

'What?' she asked, aware that he was watching her.

'It's lovely to see you letting go,' he said.

'Are you saying I'm uptight?'

'No. More that you hide yourself. But tonight you're *la belle étoile*.'

Her schoolgirl French was enough to let her translate: he thought she was a beautiful star?

She realised she'd spoken aloud when he stole a kiss. 'Right now you're shining. And you're beautiful.'

Tears pricked her eyelids. 'Thank you. *Merci beaucoup*.'

'*Je t'en prie*,' he said, and spun her round so they could salsa together, holding her close enough at times so she could feel his arousal pressing against her, and at others standing facing her and shimmying along with her.

The DJ changed to playing slower, sultrier music, and they ended up swaying together, dancing cheek to cheek. Grace felt cherished and adored—something she wasn't used to, and something she had a nasty feeling she could find addictive.

She really had to keep it in mind that this wasn't real. Roland saw this as dating practice, nothing more. Wishing it could be otherwise was the quickest route to heartache. She needed to remember her fall-back position: being sensible, the way she always was.

When the music finally ended, they took the car back to their hotel.

'That was fantastic,' she said. 'I enjoyed that so much.'

'Me, too.'

'Obviously you know the city well.' She swallowed hard. Time for a reality check. 'I assume you've done that before?'

He shook his head. 'I've been to Paris a few times with Lynette, yes—but we didn't stay at the hotel where we are tonight and I'm not retracing our footsteps.'

Which made her feel a bit better; and she was impressed that he realised she'd been worrying about that. 'So how did you know about the dancing?'

'You want the truth?' he asked. At her nod, he laughed. 'The Internet is a wonderful thing. I looked up romantic things to do in Paris. And that one struck me as being a lot of fun.'

'It was.' And she loved the fact that he'd gone to that much trouble for her. 'Your dating skills really don't need any practice, Roland. That's absolutely the way to melt someone's heart. To think about what they might like and surprise them.'

His fingers tightened around hers. 'That's what these couple of days are about. Exploring and having fun. I'm not trying to recreate the past. This is just you and me.'

As they pulled up at the hotel, he gestured across the river. 'Look.'

'The Eiffel Tower's sparkling!' she said in delight. 'I had no idea it did that at night.'

'It sparkles on the hour,' he said.

Grace was so tempted to take a photograph of the Eiffel Tower on her phone and send it to Bella—but then her sister would call her and ask why she was in Paris, and it would get too complicated. Pushing back the wistfulness and disappointment that she couldn't share this with the one person she knew would understand how much she was enjoying the chance to travel, she said, 'This is just like I imagined Paris to be. The City of Light.'

'I'll show you more tomorrow,' he promised.

Despite what he'd said on their arrival, Grace wondered if Roland expected her to share his room that night. But he kissed her at her bedroom door. 'Good night, sweet Grace.'

It took the pressure off; but, at the same time, she felt disappointment swooping in her stomach. She lay awake, wondering if she had the nerve to walk into his room. If she did, would he open his arms to her? Or would he reject her? In the end, she didn't quite have the nerve, and she fell asleep full of regret.

The next morning, she felt a bit shy with him; but he was relaxed and easy. 'Are you up for a lot of walking?' he asked.

She nodded. 'Bring it on.'

After a breakfast of excellent coffee and the best croissants she'd ever had in her life, he took her to the Tuileries and they wandered through the pretty gardens. 'I know this is a bit touristy, but we can't miss it.'

'With you being a glass fiend, you're going to show me the pyramid at the Louvre, right?' she guessed.

He laughed. 'Not just the one everyone knows about in the courtyard. This is a bit of a whistle-stop tour. I hope you don't mind.'

'No. It's fabulous,' she said, meaning it.

They walked through the museum itself, and Grace was stunned to come across pieces of art she'd known about for years, just casually dotted through the building. It didn't seem quite real, and she pinched herself surreptitiously.

And then Roland took her to the other pyramid.

'And this is what I love, here. The perfect sym-metry of glass,' he said with a grin, and took a selfie of the two of them on his phone, standing under the inverted pyramid with a rainbow of light shining across their faces.

'You and your glass,' she teased.

From the Louvre, they walked to the Place des Vosges. 'It's the oldest planned square in the city,' he told her. 'Victor Hugo lived here when he wrote *Les Misérables*.'

It was utterly beautiful: a terrace of redbrick houses with tall windows and blue-tiled roofs, and little arcades running along the bottom storey. Grace was enchanted, and even more so when they wandered through more of the Marais district. 'This is lovely,' she said. 'All cobbled streets and medieval crooked lanes.'

'It's how Paris was before Napoleon razed most of it and built all the wide avenues and huge squares,' Roland said. 'What I like about it is the way you've got old-fashioned *boulangeries* mixed in with art galleries and wine shops and jewellery designers.'

'You could just lose yourself here,' she said.

He nodded. 'It's the best way to explore.'

They ended up at Place du Marché-Ste-Catherine, a cobblestoned square with pretty plane trees and lots of cream-coloured four-storey eighteenth-century houses. On three sides of the square there were little cafés with parasols and sunshades on; there were wrought iron benches in the centre, and a couple of buskers playing Bach on the violin.

'Time for lunch,' Grace said. 'And I'm going to order for us. Even though it's a long time since I've spoken French.'

'Sure you don't want me to help?'

'Nope. I'm going outside my comfort zone,' she said. 'And I've got you to thank for making me that brave.'

'OK,' he said. *'Allons-y.'*

Grace's schoolgirl French was just about up to ordering two coffees and quiche, though she had to resort to sign language and a lot of smiling to order the lamb's lettuce salad, and Roland couldn't help smiling. Grace was oh, so sweet. And wandering through one of the prettiest districts of Paris with her had soothed his soul.

He'd called her a beautiful star, the night before. And even in the daytime she seemed lit up. He loved the fact that she was throwing herself into the whole Parisian experience, enjoying every single moment and sharing his delight in the glorious architecture. And a corner of his heart that he'd thought would stay heavy for ever suddenly seemed lighter, just because she was with him. But he knew she wanted someone who wouldn't let her down. His track record wasn't good enough. Falling in love with Grace Faraday wouldn't be fair to either of them.

That evening, they had dinner in the Michelin-starred hotel restaurant—another treat he knew she'd enjoy as much as he did—and then he took her to the Eiffel Tower. 'This is the best way to see Paris by night,' he said, 'with all the streets lit up.'

He showed her the broad boulevards radiating outwards; the River Seine was like a black silk ribbon with its bridges lit up. 'This is the Champ de Mars,' he said, showing her the south side of the tower, 'with the military school at the end.' He pointed out the shiny gold dome of the Hôtel des Invalides, and the Trocadéro gardens.

'This is amazing,' she said. And, to his shock, she threw her arms round him and kissed him.

Time seemed to stop.

And although there were plenty of other tourists enjoying the view from the platform, he felt as if the two of them were alone in a little bubble of time and space.

When Roland finally broke the kiss, he felt almost giddy and had to keep holding her tightly. And then he recovered his customary aplomb and told her more about the tower and pointed out more of the landmarks in the city. Just because if he kept talking, then he'd be able to stop himself kissing her stupid.

Back at the hotel, he had to damp down the urge to carry her across the threshold and straight to his bed. That wasn't the deal. And, even though he was pretty sure she wouldn't say no, it wouldn't be fair to her. So he kissed her good night at the doorway to her room—making very sure he kept the kiss short enough so it didn't play havoc with his self-control—and went to bed alone.

And he spent the next couple of hours lying awake, thinking of Grace.

What if she was the one who really could make him live again?

But the biggest question was, what did she want? And, if they did try to make a go of things, would their relationship splinter in the same way that his marriage had? Would she want children, to the point where nothing else mattered?

It was a risk. And he wasn't sure he had the strength left to take that risk.

So he'd stick to the rules.

Despite the fact that he really wanted to break them.

CHAPTER EIGHT

HOW DID YOU sweep someone off their feet without losing your own head in the process? Roland
still didn't have any clearer ideas the next morning. But after breakfast he took Grace to Montmartre. As he expected, she was charmed by the
gorgeous Art Deco Métro signs, loved the beautiful church and the amazing views over the city,
and enjoyed walking through the crowded square
where the artists sold their wares and did char-
coal portraits of tourists. He got her to pose on
the steps next to the funicular railway and took a
photograph of her; when a passing couple offered
to take a photograph of them together, he enjoyed
the excuse to wrap his arm round her shoulders
and for her to wrap her arm round his waist.

They stopped at one of the street vendors for a
cinnamon crêpe, then wandered further through

Montmartre, looking for the plaques to show where the famous turn-of-the-century artists had once lived or painted.

'Bella would love it here,' Grace said.

And for a moment Roland could imagine the two of them coming here with Hugh and Bella, Tarquin and Rupert, lingering at a table outside one of the cafés and talking and laughing until the early hours of the morning.

He shook himself. That wasn't going to happen. His next step was dating again, not finding his true love. And who was to say that he would find The One? Maybe one chance was all you got, and he'd already had that with Lynette. Wanting a second chance was greedy. And he had to look at it from Grace's point of view, too; even if he wanted to try making a go of things with her, she wasn't ready to rush into another long-term relationship.

So he kept it light and fun and did touristy things with her for the rest of the afternoon until it was time to catch the Eurostar back to London. This time their journey was swift and businesslike rather than slow and romantic, the way the Orient Express had been. Which was a good thing, because the brisk and businesslike feeling would stop him doing something stupid.

'Thank you, Roland,' she said when they were back in Docklands. 'I've had the nicest time ever.'

'My pleasure,' he said, meaning it.

He used the excuse of catching up with work for Friday evening and the whole of Saturday, in an attempt to cool his head again; but on Sunday afternoon, when she diffidently suggested that maybe they could go to the Science Museum in search of the seaweed 'plank', he found himself agreeing. And again he ended up holding hands with her as they walked round.

Disappointingly, they couldn't find the plank.

'Let's go next door,' he said.

'Because you want to see the dinosaurs? Or because it's one of the most gorgeous buildings in London and you want to drool over the architecture?' she asked.

He loved it when she teased him like this. Grace really seemed to get who he was and what made him tick. 'Both?' he suggested.

'Pfft. It's the brickwork all the way, with you,'

she said with a grin. 'But let's go and see the dinosaurs as well, because I loved those when I was a child.'

'And I bet you used to count the bones,' he teased back.

'Absolutely. And I could always talk Dad into getting a dinosaur head on a stick for Bella and me—you know, the sort with a trigger on the end so you can make the mouth snap shut. We used to pretend to be T-Rexes and chase each other round the garden. Bellasaurus and Graciesaurus, that was us.'

Grace, all young and carefree and letting herself shine. When had that stopped? he wondered. He'd really, really liked the carefree Grace who'd danced the salsa with him on the banks of the Seine. Could she be that Grace back in London? And could she take a risk with him?

When they queued up to see the dinosaurs, the little girl in front of them was scared when one of the large animatronic dinosaurs roared unexpectedly, and burst into tears. Her father immediately swung her up in his arms to comfort her.

'Poor little lass,' Grace said.

Roland gave her a sidelong look. Was he being oversensitive and paranoid, or did she have the same kind of broody expression that he'd seen permanently on Lynette in that last year?

'Do you want children?' The question was out before he could stop it.

She stared at him and blinked. 'That's a bit abrupt. Why do you ask?'

'Just wondering.' Stupid, stupid. Why hadn't he kept his mouth shut?

'I don't know,' she said.

'But you were engaged to Howard for four years. Surely you talked about having a family?' He knew he should shut up and leave the subject well alone, but his mouth was running away with him. Big time.

'Actually, no,' she said. 'We didn't. What about you? Did you and Lynette…?'

The question made him flinch inwardly, but he knew it was his own fault. He'd been the one to raise the subject. 'I was still getting my business off the ground.' That was true. Up to a point. But oh, yes, Lynette had wanted a baby. More than anything.

'But did you want to have children when the business was more settl—?' She stopped herself. 'Sorry. I'm probably bringing back difficult stuff for you.'

Yes, she was, but not in the way she thought. Roland had never spoken to anyone about the way he and Lyn had struggled and struggled, and how their love had got lost somewhere under her desperate need for a child. Or about the shock news the doctor had given him at the hospital. 'It's OK,' he said. Even though it wasn't and it hurt like hell.

'Sorry, anyway,' she said, and squeezed his hand.

Change the subject. Change it now, he told himself.

But it was like prodding a bruise to see if it was getting better yet. And the words just spilled out before he could stop them. 'I can imagine you as a mum.' She'd bring her child somewhere like here, to point out the wonders of the big blue whale and the dinosaurs and the fossilised lightning and the beautiful colours of the gemstones. And he had a sudden vision of himself at the seaside, building sandcastles with a little girl who had her mother's earnest blue eyes and shy smile.

'I think I'd like to be a mum,' she said.

And that was the sticking point.

Roland had wanted to be a dad—but not at the expense of his marriage. He'd wanted their life to grow and expand, not for some of it to be excluded.

'But there are no guarantees,' she said.

It was the last thing he'd expected her to say and it surprised him into asking, 'What do you mean, no guarantees?'

'Apart from the fact that I'd need to find someone I wanted to have a family with in the first place, not everyone can have children. I've got friends who couldn't, even after several rounds of IVF,' she said.

That figured. Grace would take the sensible, measured point of view. But then again, he'd thought that Lyn would take that point of view, too, and maybe look at alternative options when things hadn't gone to plan. But, once her biological clock had started ticking, Lyn's views had changed. She'd become obsessive, almost. And, instead of running away and hiding in work, he should've done more to help her. He should've found a middle way that worked for both of them.

'Not everyone can,' he said, and hoped that Grace couldn't hear the crack in his voice, the way that he could.

She didn't comment on the fact he was quiet for the rest of the afternoon, but she bought him an ice cream in the museum café, and she got him talking about the amazing architecture of the Natural History Museum.

Funny how she understood him so well and knew what was balm to his soul.

'I never thought to look it up,' she said, 'but is there a museum of architecture?'

'Actually, there's something really amazing here in London,' he said. 'It's the house of Sir John Soane—the architect who designed the Bank of England, and the Royal Hospital in Chelsea. He arranged for the house to become a museum for students and people who loved architecture, after his death. They do candlelit tours in the evening so you get the feel of what life was like there, nearly two hundred years ago.'

He smiled at her. 'Actually, if there's one next week, would you like to go?'

'Yes, but haven't you been there already?'

'Several times,' he said, 'but I see something new every time I go. It's a total maze of rooms with all these hidden compartments and corridors. The collection's arranged by pattern and symmetry rather than by period, and it's a total magpie's nest—everything from Egyptian relics to old clocks and period furniture and incredible art.' And it would be nice to share it with someone. Someone who understood what made him tick.

She smiled back. 'Sold.'

'Great.'

They visited the shop on the way out; Roland used the excuse that he wanted to pick up something for his five-year-old niece, but when Grace wasn't looking he secretly bought one of the dinosaur heads on a stick she'd told him about. Later that evening, he wrote a note on the outside of the paper bag and sneaked it into her briefcase, hoping she'd enjoy it when she found it.

* * *

On Monday morning, Grace opened her briefcase at her desk and discovered an unfamiliar paper bag resting on the top of her things.

In Roland's precise handwriting was a note.

Saw this and thought of you. Rrrr.

Intrigued, she opened the bag, and she burst out laughing when she saw the dinosaur head on a stick.

It was the last thing she would've expected from the man she'd met at Bella's wedding. But the Roland she'd got to know over the last few days had a keen sense of humour—and he made her feel more light-hearted and carefree than anyone she'd ever met. Like the teenager she'd never really been, because she'd always been the serious type.

Roland made her feel different.

And she liked that feeling.

Smiling, she texted him.

Thanks for the T-Rex. Am sure it will scare the numbers into behaving.

On impulse, she added a kiss to the end of the message, and sent it before she could chicken out.

Pleasure, came the immediate response.

Checked and is candlelit evening at museum tomorrow. Entry limited to first two hundred so we need to be there by five p.m. latest. Can you make it? R x

The fact that he'd sent her a kiss at the end of his own text made her heart flutter. It would be so easy to lose her heart to him. But that wasn't what he was looking for, and she needed to remember that. This was their last week together. They'd just enjoy it, and part as…well, hopefully, friends.

On Tuesday evening, Roland met Grace at Lincoln's Inn Fields and they joined the queue— early enough to guarantee their admission, to his relief.

He took her to the catacombs in the crypt, so she could see the sarcophagus by candlelight; there was lots of dramatic up-lighting. 'This is the spooky bit,' he said. 'It always feels like being in the middle of a gothic novel.'

'Your architect liked drama, then,' she said. 'I can't believe this is all a private collection. Imagine living here with this in your basement.'

'And this is probably how he would've lit it,' he said.

She shivered. 'It's a little bit too spooky for me.'

'Come and see my favourite bit,' he said, and took her to the model room.

'Oh, I can see why you love this,' she said with a smile.

'My favourite one is the Pantheon. I loved the model, when I was a child—and then, when I visited the real thing in Rome, I was totally blown away by it. I think it's my favourite building in the whole world.'

'So what is it about it that grabs you most?' she asked.

'The dome. It still amazes me how they constructed that dome nearly two thousand years ago, without all the modern equipment we have now. It's the most incredible feat of engineering.'

'It's impressive,' she agreed.

'I used to come here a lot when I was a student,' he said. 'Soane used to open these rooms up to his students before and after lectures, so they could get more of a feel for the subject. I could just imagine being taught architecture here with these models.' He guided her round to see the miniature Parthenon. 'These models are incredible. Even the acanthus leaves on the Corinthian capitals here are accurate copies of the real thing. It's like being on a mini Grand Tour.'

'Have you actually done the Grand Tour?' she asked.

'I did think about doing it, the year I graduated,' he admitted, 'but a real Grand Tour could last anything from several months to several years. That wasn't really an option if I wanted to get my career up and running, so I did the whistlestop version, concentrating on Italian architecture and pretty much missing out the art and sculpture.'

'What was your favourite building? After the Pantheon, that is,' she added.

'The Coliseum's a close second,' he said, 'and the Duomo in Florence is something else, especially if you go inside the dome.'

'So would you think about building something with a dome?'

'Maybe.' He smiled at her. 'I guess I could pitch to Dad and Will that we ought to have a folly—as in a mini Pantheon—in the grounds, but I have a feeling they'd both laugh until they collapsed.'

'I thought your family supported your architecture?'

'The serious stuff, they do. A mini Pantheon is pure fantasy.' He laughed. 'And if they actually let me do it, in two hundred years' time people would point at it and refer to me as Roland "the Mad Architect" Devereux. Though I guess it'd make us stand out from the crowd if we could offer weddings held in the English Pantheon.'

'I have a nasty feeling that I could be a bad influence on you,' she said.

He tightened his fingers around hers. 'And that's probably a good thing.'

* * *

They'd planned to go to the cinema the following evening; but at lunchtime Grace found a text on her phone from Roland.

Sorry, something's come up at work. I need to sort it out. Going to be late home. Can we take a rain check on the movie?

Sure, she texted back, burying her disappointment. She knew he wouldn't cancel without a good reason, and he'd given her as much notice as he could.

She texted him just before she left the office.

Have makings of stir-fry in fridge, so if you don't get time to eat I can cook you something in five minutes flat tonight.

It was a while before he replied to thank her, and he didn't get home until almost nine.

'Sit down and I'll make you a drink. Have you eaten?' she asked.

'No. I'm too tired to eat,' he admitted.

'You need to eat,' she said, and ushered him to the kitchen table. 'Give me five minutes.'

As she'd promised, five minutes later, there was a plate of chicken, stir-fry veg, sweet chilli sauce and noodles in front of him.

'Thank you. This is good,' he said after the first mouthful.

'You're very welcome. Did you manage to get your problem sorted out?' she asked.

He sighed. 'We're getting there. It's a problem with an eco extension we're doing. The team started digging foundations this morning and it turns out there's an old well shaft right in the middle of the new build site. It wasn't on any of the plans of the area, so we need to talk to the building regs inspector and the planning department about how we're going to deal with it. We can cap it and build over it, or we can make a feature of it say with a partial glass floor, but either way it's going to affect how we deal with the foundations.' He grimaced. 'I'm probably going to be tied up dealing with this until the weekend, and it means I'll be working late as well. Sorry,

Grace. It isn't what we agreed and I feel bad that I'm letting you down.'

'It's not your fault,' she said, 'and it's clearly not something you can delegate so it's fine. I can amuse myself.'

'Thank you.' He reached over to take her hand and squeezed it. 'I really appreciate you being so understanding. And don't worry about cooking for me for the rest of the week. I'll grab something with the team.'

'If there's anything you need, just tell me,' she said.

The rest of the week dragged. Grace was shocked to realise how quickly she'd come to look forward to her dates with Roland. So maybe his problem at work was a good thing; it would bring her common sense back and stop her making a fool of herself by falling for him.

On Friday evening, she went to the flat after work to see how things were going and pick up any post, and discovered there was a letter waiting for her. The job she'd been interviewed for on the day of the flood was hers, and they wanted her to start the week after next.

Given that she'd resigned herself to having to keep looking for a job, she was thrilled by the news. She texted Bella swiftly.

Got the job. Celebrate when you get back. Love you lots. x

And then she called her parents.

'Oh, darling, that's wonderful,' her mother said. 'I'm so pleased for you.'

'Can I take you and Dad out to dinner tonight to celebrate?' she asked.

'That's so lovely of you,' her mother said, 'but your dad's booked us a surprise break and we're heading out to the airport in about ten minutes. But we'll take you out the day we get back.'

'OK. That'll be lovely,' Grace said, swallowing her disappointment. 'Hey. I'd better let you go and finish getting ready. Have a great time, and text me to let me know you arrived safely.'

'We will. Love you, Gracie,' her mother said. 'And I'm so proud of you.'

'Love you, too, Mum,' Grace said.

She tried calling her three closest friends, just in case any of them might be free to celebrate her news with her, but their phones were all switched through to voicemail. By the time she got back to Docklands, Grace was feeling just a bit flat; she had some seriously good news, but nobody to celebrate with. For the first time since she'd broken up with Howard, she felt really alone.

And it made her question all her decisions. Had she done the right thing in cancelling her wedding? Should she have settled for a man who was kind but made her feel like part of the furniture?

She shook herself. No. Of course not. She'd done the right thing for both of them. She and Howard hadn't loved each other enough, and eventually they would've made each other miserable. She just had to get used to her new life. And she had a new job to look forward to—a challenge to meet. Everything was going to be just fine.

'Nothing fazes a Faraday girl,' she reminded herself out loud.

She knew Roland was busy, but texted the news

to him anyway. He didn't reply, and she was cross with herself for being disappointed that he hadn't even had time to text her back saying 'congrats'. Talk about being an ungrateful, needy brat. 'Get a grip,' she told herself crossly, 'and stop being so selfish.'

Half an hour later, the doorbell rang. A woman stood on the doorstep, holding a gorgeous hand-tied floral arrangement and three helium balloons.

'Grace Faraday?' she asked.

Grace blinked. 'Yes.'

'These are for you.' The woman—who looked strangely familiar, even though Grace knew they hadn't met before—handed her the flowers and balloons. She opened the card to find a message from Roland saying, *Well done! Congrats. R x.*

'That's amazing,' she said. 'How can he arrange something as gorgeous as this at such short notice—especially as practically everywhere is shut at this time of night?'

The delivery woman said drily, 'Because if your sister's a florist, you can talk her into doing things out of hours.' She looked Grace straight in the eye. 'He's kept you very quiet. I had no idea he was even seeing someone, let alone *living* with someone.'

This was Roland's little sister? 'You're Philly?' Grace asked, shocked.

'Phyllida Devereux of Philly's Flowers,' she confirmed.

Now Grace realised why the woman had looked familiar. Because she looked like Roland; she had the same dark eyes and the same gorgeous smile.

And Philly thought that Grace was living with Roland? Oh, help. She needed to do some damage limitation. Fast. 'We're not living together. This isn't what you think.'

Philly tipped her head to one side. 'Care to try me with an explanation?'

Roland wasn't here but, from the way he'd spoken about Philly, Grace was pretty sure they were close. 'Look, if you're not already on your way somewhere, come in for coffee and I'll explain.'

'All right.' Philly followed her inside.

Grace played for time while she made coffee. 'Have you eaten yet tonight?'

'No.'

'Then, if you're free, why don't you stay and have dinner with me?' She rummaged in the fridge. 'Do you like gnocchi with tomato and mascarpone sauce? I apologise in advance that it's shop-bought rather than home-made.'

Philly smiled. 'It sounds lovely—and Ro never cooks anyway. If I come here, either he orders something in or he makes me cook for us.'

'And I guess at least this is quick.'

'Is there anything I can do?' Philly asked.

'Lay the table?' Grace suggested, pretty sure that Roland's sister knew her way around the kitchen.

'Deal,' Philly said.

Ten minutes later, they were sitting at Roland's kitchen table with dinner in front of them.

'All righty. I'm not living with Roland—I'm staying in his guest room,' Grace said. 'I'm Bella's sister. There was a burst pipe in my flat—which used to be hers—and Bel left me Roland's number in case of emergency. He said if something like that had happened to you, he knew Hugh and Tarq would look after you, so he was going to do the same for me, as I'm Hugh's sister-in-law. And he offered me a place to store my stuff and stay until my flat dries out.'

'I get that's why you're staying here, but what I *don't* get is why he's sending you flowers.' Philly flapped a dismissive hand. 'Well, obviously as he asked for helium balloons that said "New Job" and "Congratulations" and I wrote the message on the card, I realise you've just got a new job. But this is my brother we're talking about and he hasn't sent a woman flowers since—' She stopped and narrowed her eyes. 'I assume you *know*?'

'About what happened to Lynette? Yes, he told me,' Grace said.

Philly looked thoughtful. 'And it's something he doesn't talk about very much. So are you seeing each other?'

How could she explain? 'It's complicated,' Grace prevaricated.

Philly folded her arms. 'Which tells me nothing. Spill, or I'll make his life a misery until you do—and, trust me, only little sisters can be that annoying.'

Grace smiled. 'Mine isn't annoying. She's lovely.'

'I can be lovely. But I'm definitely the annoying variety,' Philly said. 'Explain complicated.'

'We're helping each other out for a few weeks. Which are practically at an end.'

Philly frowned. 'What do you mean by helping each other out? And why is there a time limit?'

Grace knew that this was going to sound bad. 'He's practising his dating skills on me.'

Philly looked suspicious. 'And what do you get out of it?'

'Being swept off my feet.'

'And what happens at the end of these few weeks? You're going to be just good friends?' Philly added quote marks with her fingers round the last phrase.

Grace felt herself blush. 'Yes.'

'And you'd swear that in court?'

'I'd swear that he doesn't think of me romantically.'

Bad move. Because Philly honed straight in on what Grace hadn't said. 'But *you* think of *him* that way.'

'It's not going to happen,' Grace said. 'I went into this with my eyes open. To be honest, although he says he wants to start dating again, I think he's still in love with Lynette. But if I can help him take those first steps into coming back unto the world, then I'm glad I can do that.'

'You're in love with him,' Philly said.

'We barely know each other. We only met briefly at Hugh's wedding and we've known each other a little over two weeks,' Grace protested. But she had a nasty feeling that Philly was right. Even though it wasn't the sensible thing to do, she'd let herself fall for Roland. A man who wasn't available. Which was as stupid as it got.

'A little over two weeks is long enough.' Philly paused. 'He's seemed different whenever I've talked to him recently. Now I know why. I think you might be good for him.'

'It's not going to happen,' Grace repeated. 'I'm not what he's looking for.' And, even though a part of her really wished that she could be what Roland was looking for, she was sensible enough to know that she didn't fit into his world. She wasn't glamorous and exciting; she was sensible and slightly dull.

* * *

Philly had left by the time Roland returned, that evening.

'Thank you for the flowers and balloons,' Grace said.

'My pleasure.' He inspected them. 'Philly did a good job.'

'I like your sister.' Grace paused. 'I hope you don't mind, but she stayed for dinner.'

'And interrogated you?' he asked wryly.

'To be fair, she was delivering flowers to a woman at your house. If I'd been in her shoes, I would've been asking questions, too.' She smiled. 'Philly's nice.'

'Yeah, she is.' He paused. 'What did you tell her?'

'That you're putting me up while the flat dries out.'

'And she didn't ask anything else?' He looked sceptical.

Best to admit the truth, Grace thought. 'She did. So I told her about our deal.'

'Uh-huh.'

She wasn't going to tell him about what Philly

had guessed. Because that was way outside the terms of their deal and he didn't need to know about that. 'She gets it. I think she's glad you're...' She grimaced. 'Sorry. That's not tactful.'

'Planning to get back in the land of the living,' he said. 'It's fine. I'm sorry I was working and couldn't take you out tonight to celebrate your new job. The flowers were sort of an apology as well as a congratulations.'

'The flowers are absolutely lovely,' she said.

'And Bella's away, so you couldn't celebrate with her.'

'And my parents are going on holiday; they're on their way to the airport now. Plus my friends are all busy. So, actually, I was pretty glad that your sister came round,' she admitted. 'It stopped me feeling completely like Billy-No-Mates.'

'I intend to make this up to you tomorrow—that is, if it's not going to mess up any plans you've made?' he asked.

She shook her head. 'We agreed to keep ourselves free until Hugh and Bella got back, so I haven't made any plans.'

'Good. It's going to be an early start, so can you be ready for six?'

'Sure.'

'Pack for a night away. Nothing bigger than a case you can take in the cabin of a plane. Shoes you can walk in, something dressy, a hat, sunglasses and your passport. And don't ask where we're going.'

'Because you're not going to tell me.'

'Humour me. I want to see your face when we get there.' He wrapped his arms round her. 'Congrats again. I knew you'd do it.'

'Thank you.' She hugged him back. Funny how the world felt all right again when he was this close to her. But she'd have to get used to being on her own from next week onwards. So she needed to start putting that little bit of distance between them from now on.

CHAPTER NINE

THE NEXT MORNING, Grace was ready to leave at six. And Roland refused to tell her anything about where they were going until they were at the airport and their flight was called.

'We're going to Venice?' Her eyes grew wide in wonder. 'You're taking me to Venice just for the *day*?'

'And night,' he corrected. 'We fly back to London late tomorrow afternoon.'

'Venice,' she said again, seeming unable to quite take it in.

'It's my favourite place in the world,' he said.

Then he saw the wariness creep into her expression. He could guess why. 'Yes, I've been there a few times with Lyn,' he said, 'but you're not going to be following in her footsteps. This is just you and me. We're celebrating your new job.'

The beginning of her new life. And ending their deal on a high note. He didn't say it, but he was pretty sure she was thinking it, too. He was sticking to the plan. Sweeping her off her feet—and then saying goodbye.

Venice.

Who else but Roland would think about going to Venice just for one night? Grace thought.

And she had a feeling that he'd planned this right from the beginning, when she'd first told him that she hadn't travelled much. It would be the perfect end to their perfect few weeks together.

She was very aware that tomorrow was the last day of their agreement. And, as soon as Bella came back from honeymoon and discovered what had happened with the burst pipe, no doubt she'd insist that Grace came to stay with her and Hugh until the flat was habitable again. There was no reason for Grace to remain at Roland's house.

Unless he asked her to stay.

Somehow, she didn't think that was going to happen. Roland's job meant that he was used to planning in advance and working to a schedule. This was no different, really. It had been a short-term project to brush up his dating skills and sweep her off her feet. Mission accomplished, just before the deadline.

So she'd just enjoy this weekend for what it was.

The end.

Roland held her hand all the way on the plane, and when he walked with her to the end of the jetty at the airport. 'I thought we could take a water taxi into the city,' he said. 'It's the best way to see Venice for the first time.'

Once they were on the lagoon, Grace understood why he'd suggested bringing a hat and sunglasses. The reflections of the sun on the water were so bright that she would've been squinting without them. 'Right now, I feel like a princess,' she said.

'That's the idea,' he said. 'Watch the horizon.'

The water was pure turquoise and she couldn't make anything out at first. But then she saw rooflines, all spires and domes. As they drew closer, she could see that there were houses packed in tightly along the shoreline, with bridges arching over the entrances to the waterways running through the city.

'Venice rising from the water—this is one of the most beautiful things I've ever seen,' she whispered.

Roland's fingers tightened around hers. 'And it gets better. Watch.'

As they grew closer, she could see the architecture more clearly. There were shutters at the windows of the houses; plaster peeled away from some of the brickwork, while other houses looked as if they'd been recently restored.

Their driver took them under a bridge, and now they were really in Venice.

'I've never been in a city without any traffic noise, before,' she said. And it was odd to hear the swish of the waves and hear people talking where she'd usually expect to hear engines revving and horns blasting.

'What's that building?' she asked. 'All that latticed plaster reminds me of the icing on a wedding cake.'

'That's the Palazzo Ducale—the Doge's Palace,' he said. 'And that tall tower opposite—the one with the red bricks and green roof—is Galileo's Tower.' He smiled at her. 'We'll walk through St Mark's Square later, so you can have a closer look at them.'

'Thank you,' she said. Coming here was a treat—but coming here with someone who knew the place and could help her to find all the most interesting bits was better still. And the fact that that someone was Roland...

When their driver moored at the jetty, Roland helped her from the boat.

'I still can't get over this,' she said. 'I've seen documentaries and photographs of Venice in magazines, but the real thing is beyond anything I'd dreamed about. I think,' she added shyly, 'I like this even more than Paris.'

He looked pleased. 'I hoped you'd like this. Let's check in, and then we can go exploring.'

The hotel was part of an old palazzo; the decor was all cream and navy and gold, with marble flooring and a fountain in the reception area. Roland had booked them a suite with two rooms. Because they were only staying for one night,

Grace managed to unpack her overnight case very swiftly.

The streets outside were crowded, yet at the same time it was so much quieter than she was used to in London, without the traffic noises. Gondolas and small rowing boats glided through the narrow canals; there were bridges everywhere, with the sunlight reflecting off the water and dappling the undersides of the bridges.

Shops crowded against each other, offering glass and Venetian masks and marbled paper; tourists posed for photographs on the bridges and in the little squares. 'All the signs seem to point either to the Rialto or San Marco,' she said in surprise.

'In this part of the city, they're the two main destinations and all the streets lead to them—though sometimes it's the long way round,' he said with a smile. 'Let's start at the Rialto. There's a gorgeous view of the Grand Canal from the bridge.'

The marble on the bridge had been worn shiny by countless hands skimming across it; and Grace leaned against the bridge to watch the traffic on the canal go by. When they finished crossing the bridge to go into the marketplace itself, she discovered that it was a sheer delight, full of colour—selling everything from fresh seafood glistening in the sunlight through to tiny wild strawberries and fragrant herbs sold by the handful.

'This is amazing,' she said.

He glanced at his watch. 'Wait a second.'

And then suddenly bells were pealing all over the city.

'Is it a special occasion, or does this happen every day?' she asked.

'Every day. In the summer it's like aural sunlight; in the winter, especially if it's foggy, it's a little spooky,' he said.

'I can see why Venice is one of your favourite places,' she said. 'It's amazing.'

They walked hand in hand through the narrow streets, enjoying all the bustle around them and stopping to buy a *piadina* from one of the street vendors to keep them going over lunchtime. Grace stopped to take photographs of the figures outside some of the mask shops—the terrifying plague doctor with his hooked beak, and the pretty harlequin—and took a selfie of Roland and herself standing on a bridge with a gondola gliding behind them. 'Do you mind me being horribly touristy?' she asked.

'Not a bit.' He smiled. 'Actually, I'm enjoying seeing how much you like Venice.'

'It's gorgeous,' she said. 'I know I keep saying it, but it's like... Venice is just like nowhere else I've ever been.'

'If you don't mind us doing a whistlestop tour,' he said, 'we can go take a look at the basilica and the Doge's Palace.'

'But you've seen it all before,' she said.

He shrugged. 'You know I never pass up the opportunity to look at architecture. And besides, you can't come to Venice and not see the *quadriga*—the four horses. They've been in Venice for more than eight hundred years.'

Grace thoroughly enjoyed their tour of the cathedral and the palace, especially as Roland turned out to be a mine of information about the buildings. And she loved the fact that he took a selfie of them on the loggia of the basilica, next to the replicas of the four bronze horses.

Right now, she thought wistfully, this felt like a honeymoon. Though she knew she was being ridiculous. Roland hadn't given her any signals that he wanted their relationship to continue past their agreement, let alone anything more. They'd known each other for only a few weeks; it was way, way too soon to fall in love.

Stop being greedy, she reminded herself. Just enjoy every second of this and stop wishing for something you're not going to get.

'I thought we'd have dinner early,' he said, 'because there's something else you absolutely have to do in Venice.'

'Bring it on,' Grace said with a smile.

Roland found a little tucked away restaurant. 'My Italian's a bit scrappy,' he said, 'but I can get by. What would you like to eat?'

'A Venetian speciality,' she said.

'Let's ask the waiter what he recommends,' he said. 'But for pudding I'd say it has to be tiramisu in the area where it was invented.'

The waiter recommended *sarde in saor*—sardines in a sweet and sour sauce—followed by *polenta e schie*—tiny Venetian shrimps on a bed of white polenta. And the tiramisu was the best Grace had ever, ever tasted.

'This is perfect,' she said. 'Thank you so much.'

But the best was what Roland had arranged for after coffee.

'I wanted to eat early,' he said, 'so we'd get to see the sunset.'

And then she discovered where he'd planned their viewpoint to be: from the seat of a gondola.

Their gondolier wore the traditional black trousers, striped jersey and straw hat; he guided them through the narrow waterways, using his pole to propel them and pushing his body against it to help them turn the odd corner. To Grace's delight he actually serenaded them in a mellow tenor voice.

The sunset itself was the most romantic thing she'd ever seen: the sun sinking, the sky turning shades of orange and apricot with the domes and towers of the city silhouetted against it, and the turquoise waters of the Grand Canal changing to reflect the deep tones of the sky.

She was too moved to say a word; she leaned her head against Roland's shoulder, drinking in the view and enjoying his nearness. He held her close, and again this felt so much like a honeymoon.

The gondolier took them through the narrow waterways again, which had turned almost inky to reflect the darkened sky; reflections from little globe-shaped lamps flickered on the water. 'This is so pretty,' she said. 'Thank you so much.'

'My pleasure,' he said, and stole a kiss.

They lapsed back into companionable silence; then, as a covered walkway rose in front of them, Roland said, 'This is the Bridge of Sighs. It's traditional to kiss underneath it.'

What else could she do but kiss him as the gondola glided underneath the bridge?

'This was the perfect end to a perfect evening,' she said as the gondolier tied up the boat at the jetty by St Mark's Square and helped them off the gondola.

'We haven't finished quite yet,' Roland said. 'Remember tangoing by the Seine? Now we're going to do the same in St Mark's Square. Well, not necessarily dance the tango—it depends what they're playing.'

As they walked into the square, lit by more of the pretty globe-shaped lights, Grace realised what he meant. There were tables and chairs outside Florian's and Quadri's, the two oldest *caffès* in the city, and a couple of small bands played on stages underneath gazebos.

Roland spun her into his arms and began to dance with her. Other couples were doing the same, she noticed, so instead of protesting that they were going to make a spectacle of themselves, she relaxed and gave herself up to the sheer pleasure of being held by Roland.

Grace looked so beautiful in the soft light of the square, Roland thought. Tonight, she was really shining—relaxed, happy, enjoying the music and the dancing and the sheer romance that was Venice.

And he, too, was being seduced by the place. To the point that when they got back to the hotel and he'd unlocked the door to their suite, he actually picked her up and carried her across the threshold.

Then he realised what he was doing, and set her back down on her feet. 'Sorry. I got a bit carried away.'

She smiled and reached up to stroke his face. 'I think you were doing the carrying. Literally. And the answer's yes.'

He sucked in a breath. Was she saying…? 'But—'

She pressed a finger lightly against his lips. 'No strings,' she said. 'That's what we agreed. And tonight's just you and me and Venice.'

'Are you sure about this?' he asked.

Her eyes were almost navy in the low light. 'I'm very sure.'

'Grace, you don't owe me anything. I didn't bring you here expecting you to sleep with me in exchange for the trip.'

'I know, and that's not why I'm saying yes.' She took a deep breath. 'It's because I want to. I know there are no strings and this is just temporary between you and me—but you've swept me off my feet this far, so let's go the whole way.'

He needed no further encouragement. He picked her up and carried her across the threshold to his bedroom.

And then he got to live out the dream he'd had the previous weekend. Unzipping her dress, sliding it off her shoulders, kissing every centimetre of skin he revealed—and finally losing himself in her warm sweet depths.

That night he fell asleep with his arms wrapped round her and her arms wrapped round him, feeling more at peace with himself than he had in way too long.

The next morning, Roland woke first. Guilt flooded through him. He really had let the romance of Venice carry off his common sense, last night. Even though Grace had told him that she was sure, he shouldn't have let things go this far.

So what now? Would her feelings have changed this morning? Would she regret it? Would she want things to be different? Or would they both be able to blame it on the romance of the sunset and the music?

She was shy with him when she woke, and he knew he had to break the ice.

'I'm sorry,' he said. 'I, um…I guess last night shouldn't have happened. I apologise.'

'Don't apologise. It was just as much my idea as yours,' she said. 'It wasn't part of our deal. We got carried away by—well, by Venice. So we can pretend it didn't happen.'

If she'd wanted last night to be the start of something more, now was the perfect time to say so. The fact that she hadn't made it clear to him that she intended to stick to the terms of their arrangement.

So today was their very last day together.

This was going to be goodbye.

As far as he knew, the landlord hadn't contacted her any more about the situation with the flat, so she might still need to be his house guest for a while. But Bella and Hugh were due back from their honeymoon tomorrow, and it was more than likely that as soon as Bella learned what had happened, she would insist on Grace moving in with her.

And then he and Grace would be polite and distant strangers.

That was what they'd agreed, so why did it make him feel so antsy?

'I, um— There was something I wanted to show you this morning,' he said. 'Shall we go exploring straight after breakfast?'

'That sounds good,' she agreed.

A shower helped him get some of his equilibrium back. Strong Italian coffee helped even more.

And then, with the help of a map, he found the Sotoportego dei Preti. 'This is what I wanted to show you,' he said. 'It's the *cuore in mattone*— the heart in the brick.'

'I should've guessed it would be something architectural,' she said with a smile, looking at the brick just below the lintel. 'A heart-shaped brick is very appropriate for Venice. What's the story behind it?'

'You're meant to touch it and make a wish—so the legend goes, if your wish is respectful and harms no one, it will be answered within the year,' he said.

'So have you known about this for years, or was this like the tangoing in Paris?'

'Like the tangoing. I looked it up on the Internet,' he admitted. 'Shall we?'

They touched the brick together and made a wish. Roland couldn't help asking, 'So what did you wish for?'

'I imagine it's like the wish you make on a star or when you blow out the candles on your birthday cake,' she said. 'So I can't tell you, or it won't come true.'

'I guess.' And that meant he didn't have to tell her what he'd wished for, either.

For love to fill his life again. For this thing between them to become real.

They took the water bus over to Murano to see all the pretty painted cottages and to see a glass-blowing demonstration.

'You and your glass,' she teased afterwards.

He spread his hands. 'You can't come to Venice without seeing glass being blown or lace-making.'

'I guess. And it was pretty spectacular—I've

never seen anything like that before. Do you mind if I take a quick look round the shop?'

'Sure. Though shopping's not really my thing, so I'm going to sit in the sun while you're looking round. Don't rush,' he added. 'Just come and find me when you're ready.'

Grace was glad that Roland wasn't planning to shadow her in the shop, because she'd hoped to find a gift for him to thank him for taking her to Venice. And there was a beautiful modern paperweight that was absolutely perfect. Better still, the sales assistant wrapped it beautifully for her, so he wouldn't have a clue about it.

Roland found a little *osteria* that sold *cicheti*— Venetian tapas—for lunch, and the choice was breathtaking: tiny *polpette*, stuffed olives, tomato bruschetta, white asparagus wrapped in pancetta, baby octopus in lemon, slices of grilled polenta with salami, *arancini*, spider crab, *zucchini* stuffed with tomatoes and cheese, and marinated artichokes. Between them, they tried a little of everything, sharing a plate and feeding each other little morsels; again, it felt like being

on a honeymoon, and Grace had to remind herself to keep her feet on the ground. To go back
to being sensible, quiet Grace.

But on the flight back to England, Roland went
quiet on her.

And that in turn gave her time to think. Today
was the last day of their arrangement. Their last
day together. Grace and Roland had agreed that
once Bella and Hugh returned tomorrow, from
then on they'd be polite strangers.

A few weeks ago, that had seemed perfectly
reasonable. But, last night, they'd made love. So
would he still want to stick to their original deal,
or would he suggest that they try to make a go
of things?

She knew what she wanted. She'd wished on
the heart-shaped brick that things would be different—that this thing between them could turn
out to be real. But she wasn't quite brave enough
to bring it up. This morning, she'd woken to find
him looking full of panic, clearly having second thoughts. What else could she have done
but pretend everything was just fine and let him
off the hook?

It was pretty clear that her feelings were one-sided. Last night, they'd simply got carried away with the romance of Venice, the gondola and dancing through St Mark's Square. It hadn't been real.

So it was better to leave this situation with her dignity intact.

And she'd get over this.

She would.

Back in the airport at London, she switched on her phone to find that it was dead. 'I must've left an app on that drained the battery,' she said.

'You can use my phone if you need to,' Roland offered.

'Thanks, but I didn't tell my family I was away so they won't be worrying. It can wait,' she said.

Back at Roland's house, there was a pile of post. He set his coffee machine working, then sat at the kitchen table to go through his mail, while Grace plugged in her phone and waited for it to charge for long enough that she could switch it on again, then checked the messages that came through.

She was about to tell Roland the good news

when she noticed that his face had blanched. 'Is everything OK?' she asked instead, concerned.

'Sure.' But he didn't move. He just sat there, staring at the table.

She finished making the coffee and brought his mug over to the table. 'You don't look sure,' she said gently.

'I...' He sighed and gestured to one of the envelopes. 'This came from Mindy, Lyn's best friend from school. They're moving house and she found these photos and thought I might like them.'

'That was kind of her,' Grace said. Or was it? He looked as if someone had ripped his heart out. Roland had clearly loved his wife deeply. Despite the fact that he'd said he was ready to move on, from his reaction to getting those photographs Grace didn't think he was. Was he feeling guilty that he'd taken her to Venice—as if he'd betrayed Lyn's memory? Though asking him would be like stomping over still-fresh wounds, and she didn't know what to say.

In the end she reached over to squeeze his hand. 'I didn't know Lyn, but you said that she wouldn't want you to be sad. Why don't you look at the photos and remember the good times?'

'I...' His voice sounded thick with emotion. 'But you...'

'We had a deal,' she said. 'It finishes today. And I'd like to think that we've become friends.' More than that—they'd been lovers, and it had shown Grace exactly what she'd been missing in her life. How wrong she'd been when she'd thought she could settle for nice enough instead of the real thing.

Roland could so easily have been her real thing.

But she knew that he wasn't ready to move on, and she wasn't sure if he ever would be.

'Friends,' he said.

'I'd like to see the photos,' she said. 'Talk to me, Roland. Tell me about Lyn. Tell me about the good times.'

Roland knew he ought to tell Grace the truth. About the bad times. But he didn't want her to think badly of Lyn. Or of him.

He took the photographs out of the envelope.

'They're from years ago. Just a weekend at the beach with friends.'

'She looks nice,' Grace said. 'As if she was fun. And you both look so happy.'

They had been. Once.

'Yeah.' His voice cracked.

Grace pushed her chair back and walked round the table to wrap her arms round him. 'Don't focus on the fact that she's gone. Focus on the fact that you were together and you loved each other.'

And it hadn't been enough. But how could he explain?

'Grace, I wish…'

As if her thoughts were totally in tune with his, she held him just that little bit tighter. 'Roland, these past few weeks have been amazing. You've swept me off my feet—but, better still, you've shown me that I don't have to settle for being sensible all the time. That it's OK to dream and to reach for those dreams. And your dating skills are just fine—but I don't think you're ready to move on. Not yet.'

No. Because his guilt still held him back, making him feel that he didn't deserve a second chance. Not when he'd messed up so badly. 'I guess,' he said.

But, even if they could get over that hurdle, there was another sticking point. The one that had cracked his marriage. He and Lyn had had trouble conceiving, and he didn't know if the problem had lain with him. What if Grace wanted children—and, just like it had happened with Lyn, their love got bogged down in the problems of conception? He couldn't bear to go through that nightmare again. And, even though he knew Grace was sensible and down to earth, even the most sensible person could be sideswiped by emotions.

He had to let this go. For her sake as well as for his own. He had to get out of her way and let her find the happiness she deserved. Even if it was with someone else.

'Those messages that came through—one was from my landlord,' she said. 'Thanks to your restoration expert sucking up the water and putting a dehumidifier in early, the flat's all dried out now. It seemed they don't need to strip the plaster back after all, so I can move my stuff back whenever I like. Which is perfect timing,' she said brightly.

Meaning she was going to walk out of his life. Roland didn't want her to go—but he knew she was right. He wasn't ready to move on. It wasn't fair to ask her to wait indefinitely.

'I'll get a couple of the guys to move the heavy stuff for you in the morning if you don't mind lending me your key,' he said.

'Thank you.'

'No problem,' he said. 'And thank you. You've helped me, too, these last few weeks.'

But not enough, Grace thought. Not enough for him to be able to move on from the sadness of his past and ask her to stay.

'Great,' she said. 'I guess I'd better start getting my stuff together—and let you get on.'

'Uh-huh.' He gave her an awkward smile. 'Let me know if you need anything.'

She did. She needed him. But it wasn't fair to put that extra burden on him. 'Sure,' she said.

'I'd better check my emails,' he said.

'Yes. So life goes back to normal tomorrow for

both of us,' she said. 'You get your space back. And I get to stand on my own two feet again.'

'Well—good night.'

'Good night. And thanks for everything.' This time, she didn't hug him—because it would hurt way too much to let him go. Instead, she had to go back to the fall-back position. Sensible Grace.

If only it could've been otherwise.

CHAPTER TEN

GRACE SPENT THE morning moving her things back to the flat. Just as Roland had promised, he'd sent a van and two of his workmen to move the heavy stuff for her, and she'd bought them both a case of beer to thank them for their help.

When she'd put the last of her things in the car, she took the gift-wrapped paperweight she'd bought in Venice from her bag and went into Roland's office. She put the parcel in the top drawer of his desk, along with the card she'd written earlier, and closed the drawer again.

Once he'd finished grieving for Lynette, he'd make someone a wonderful partner.

If only it could've been her.

But he wasn't ready to move on; and she was still up in the air after her break-up with Howard. Being the one who'd called everything off didn't mean that she'd escaped any feelings of hurt and loss. She still needed to work out what she really wanted from life.

Besides, it was way too fast for her to have fallen in love with Roland. She'd just responded to the way he'd swept her off her feet, that was all. She couldn't possibly be in love with him.

She set the alarm and locked the door behind her, then posted his door key through the letter-box. Have locked up and left your key, she texted.

Back in her own flat, she spent her time cleaning the place from top to bottom and then moving everything back into its rightful place. She called in to see Bella and Hugh with a bottle of champagne, and thought she'd managed to fool Bella into thinking that everything was fine; though the next evening her sister turned up unexpectedly, bearing a seriously good walnut cake from her local bakery.

'Spill,' Bella demanded.

Just like Roland's sister had demanded last week, Grace thought wryly.

'There's nothing to tell,' she said, giving her best fake smile.

Bella coughed. 'You look worse now than when Mrs Concrete Hair used to do a hatchet job on your confidence with her sly little insinuations. So what's happened? Has Howard had an epiphany and asked you to go back to him, and Mama Dearest has stuck her oar in?'

'No to both,' Grace said. 'And I'm not going back to Howard. We wouldn't make each other happy. And he's a nice guy, Bel. He deserves to be happy.'

'And he needs to grow a backbone, but OK,' Bella said. 'So if it's not Howard, it's someone else. You might as well tell me, Gracie, because you know I won't shut up until you do.' Bella cut them both a large piece of cake.

Grace knew that her sister meant it, so she gave in and told Bella about her deal with Roland. 'And it's fine,' she said. 'We both did what we promised. He swept me off my feet and I helped him with his dating skills. End of story. If we see each other again, we'll be polite but distant strangers.'

'Which obviously isn't what you want.'

Grace denied it, though she knew full well that Bella wasn't going to believe her.

'Just call him,' Bella said, rolling her eyes. 'Tell him how you feel. What have you got to lose?'

'Bel, he's still in love with Lynette. I can't compete with a memory,' Grace said. 'And don't get any bright ideas about inviting us both to dinner and trying to fix us up. It'll just be embarrassing. I'll be fine. I've got my new job to look forward to, and that'll keep me busy.'

And if she kept telling herself that, eventually she'd believe it.

Over the next couple of days, Roland threw himself into work and refused to admit to himself how much he missed Grace. How empty the whole place felt without Grace around.

She thought he couldn't move on because he was still in love with Lyn. It wasn't true. But he'd let her go because he came with baggage and he hadn't wanted to drag her down with it.

Had he made a mistake?

If he'd opened up to her properly, told her the whole truth instead of just parting, would she have understood? Could she have helped him start his life all over again—give him a second chance?

He shook himself. No. He was being selfish. He'd done the right thing—even though it hurt.

He tried distracting himself with a magazine. On one page, he saw a photograph of the heart-shaped brick he and Grace found in Venice. According to the paragraph beneath the photograph, Roland had got the legend completely wrong. It wasn't about wishes coming true. Allegedly, if you pressed the brick you fell in love immediately; if you pressed it together, you'd be devoted for ever.

And he and Grace had touched the brick at the same time.

A pretty story. That was all it was. He tried to put it out of his head and started on some preliminary sketches from his latest design brief. When the point of his pencil snapped, he opened his desk drawer to grab a new lead; but there was something he didn't recognise in the drawer. A wrapped parcel, next to a card. The handwriting on the envelope was Grace's. When he opened it, the card showed a picture of Venice at sunset, very similar to the one they'd seen on the gondola. Inside, she'd written, *Thank you for sweeping me off my feet.*

The parcel contained a beautiful paperweight in shades of turquoise and blue. The sort of thing he would've chosen for himself. He handled the smooth glass thoughtfully. She'd thanked him for sweeping her off her feet and she'd bought him the most perfect present.

She understood him.

Would she understand if he told her the rest? And would she be prepared to take a risk on him?

There was only one way to find out. He called her. Her phone went through to voicemail, so he assumed that she was busy. 'Grace, it's Roland. Please call me when you get this message.' He left his number, just in case she'd mislaid it.

And now it was up to her.

Why was Roland calling her? Grace wondered.

Maybe she'd left something behind and he'd just discovered it. Of course he wasn't calling her to say he'd changed his mind about the terms of their deal. It was ridiculous to hope.

When she was quite sure that she wasn't going to make a fool of herself and blurt out something inappropriate, she returned his call.

He answered on the second ring. 'Roland Devereux.' He sounded as cool and impassive as he'd been the first time she'd called him. When she'd mistakenly thought he was her landlord. And now…

'It's Grace,' she said. 'Returning your call.'

'Thank you.'

'What did you want? Did I leave something behind?' Despite her best intentions, hope flickered in her heart.

'Yes.'

The hope sputtered and died. 'Sorry. Let me know when it's convenient to come and pick it up.'

'I'll come over.'

'I can't put you to all that trouble,' she protested.

'It's no trouble. I'll be in the area anyway.'

Why? Work? But it wasn't her place to ask.

'OK. Thank you. Let me know when, and I'll make sure I'm here.'

'Now,' he suggested.

Now? As in…right *now*? Then she realised he was waiting for her answer. 'I—um, yes, sure. I guess at least this time you won't be helping me shift furniture out of a flooded flat.'

'Indeed. See you soon.'

It took all of ninety seconds for her to tidy the flat.

And then what? Would he stay for coffee? Was this the beginning of them becoming friends? *Could* they be friends, after their fling? Or would the memories always get in the way?

When the doorbell rang, her heart leapt. She took a deep breath and reminded herself to act cool, calm and collected. 'Hello, Roland,' she said as she opened the door. Then she noticed that he wasn't carrying anything. She frowned. 'I thought you said I left something behind?'

'You did.' He paused. 'Me.'

'What?' She couldn't quite process this. 'I don't understand.'

'We need to talk.'

She frowned again. 'But I thought we'd already said it all. We had an agreement. You swept me off my feet and I can rubber stamp your dating skills. And now it's all done and dusted.'

'There's a lot more to say,' he said, 'but I don't want to do it on your doorstep.'

Her head was in a whirl. 'Sorry. I'm being rude. Come in. Can I get you a drink or something?'

He shook his head. 'I just want to talk.'

She gestured to the sofa. There wasn't anywhere else to sit, unless she opted for one of the metal dining chairs at the small table in the kitchen part of the flat, so she sat next to him.

'I don't know where to start,' he admitted.

'Try the beginning,' she said. 'Or wherever you feel like starting and you can go back and forth.'

'Then I'm going to tell you something I've never told anyone—not even my family or my best friends.' He took a deep breath. 'It's about Lyn. Everyone thinks I've been mourning her for the last two years.'

'And you haven't?' she asked, surprised. But Lynette had been the love of Roland's life and he'd lost her in horrible circumstances. Of course he'd been mourning her. He didn't even have any of the wedding photographs on display in his house because it clearly hurt too much. And the way he'd reacted to the photographs Lyn's friend had sent had signalled very clearly that he was still in love with Lyn.

'More like nearly three,' he said.

He'd mourned her for a year before she'd died? But why? Grace bit her lip. 'Was she ill but you hadn't told anyone?'

'Sort of.' He sighed. 'She wanted a baby.'

Which wasn't remotely the same as being ill. Or did he mean a different sort of problem? But Roland hadn't seemed the selfish type. She didn't understand. 'I take it from that, you didn't want a baby?' Grace guessed.

'No, I did,' he said, 'but I always thought love would expand along with my family. With Lyn, it narrowed. Right from the moment we first talked about it and started trying, she changed. All her friends who started trying fell pregnant the very first month, which made it even harder for her when she didn't.'

'Did you talk to a doctor about it?'

He nodded. 'He said we were both young and they wouldn't even consider offering us fertility treatment until we'd tried for at least another year. And it broke her, Grace. Every month when her period started, it was like the end of the world. And every time we made love, it was timed by her ovulation chart. I tried taking her away for the weekend and being spontaneous to take her mind off things, but nothing worked. She was driven. It was as if our relationship was only there for the sole purpose of having a baby, and I hated that I was letting her down all the time.'

She took his hand. 'Hey. You tried. You were there for her.'

'Not enough,' he admitted, 'and that's the really shameful bit. I don't like myself very much, Grace.'

'Hey. We all have things that make us feel that way,' she said gently. 'I'm not squeaky clean, either. I broke off my engagement three weeks before the wedding day, remember?'

'Which was the right thing to do,' he said. 'Whereas I...' He sighed. 'We stopped seeing my family. Will and Susie have a little girl, Matilda, and when Lyn couldn't get pregnant she couldn't handle being around children. It made her feel a failure, even though I tried to tell her that she wasn't a failure and nobody was ever going to judge her. But I couldn't exactly explain to everyone why Lyn didn't want to be anywhere near Tilda, not without telling people the truth—and she'd sworn me to secrecy because she didn't want anyone pitying her or judging her. So we used my work as an excuse, saying I was too busy for us to see people.' He grimaced. 'My mum even rang me to say she was worried about us—she said that I was neglecting Lyn for work and she asked if she could do anything to help. I hated having to lie to my family.'

'But you weren't neglecting Lyn—you were trying to protect her,' Grace protested.

He shook his head. 'Actually, my mum was right. Because it got to the point where I was glad to have an excuse to be away. I did end up neglecting Lyn. I accepted invitations to give lectures abroad so I didn't have to face all that pain. And that's why I was away when the accident happened.'

'The accident wasn't your fault, Roland.'

'I know,' he said. 'And I keep telling myself that, even if I had been in London, the accident might still have happened. But at least then I would have been there to say goodbye to her before she died, instead of being thousands of miles away.'

'I'm sure Lyn knew that you loved her.'

He nodded. 'And I did, even though our marriage was cracking at the seams. But the very worst bit was what the doctor told me, something I couldn't bear to tell anyone because it was just so…' He caught his breath.

She squeezed his hand. 'Roland, you don't have to talk about this. And it's understandable that you're still in love with Lyn.'

'I'm not,' he said. 'I miss her. But I missed her for a year before she died. I missed the closeness of being with someone. And it's taken me a while to work through all the guilt and misery I've been feeling. I wasn't sure that I'd ever be ready to put my life back together again, but…' He drew her hand up to his mouth and kissed the backs of her fingers. 'I've worked out for myself that the only way to finally get past the pain and heal again is to talk about it. I don't want to have any secrets from you, Grace.' He closed his eyes for a moment, and her heart bled for him. He'd been through so much. 'I haven't been able to say this to anyone, because—well, I know what Lyn meant about not being able to face all the pity. I've been there. But I know you won't pity me.'

'I won't pity you,' she promised. 'But I do reserve the right to give you a hug.'

'OK.' He dragged in a breath. 'Lyn was pregnant when she died. It was so early on that she probably didn't even know. But how different things might've been,' he finished wistfully.

Roland would've been a father and Lyn would've had the baby she'd longed for so badly. And his marriage might have healed. But the driver who'd crashed into Lyn had taken away all those possibilities. No wonder Roland had locked himself away. 'I'm so sorry,' she said, still holding his hand.

'And that's partly why I haven't really dated since she died. Part of me wants to move on, because I can't spend the rest of my life in mourning. The Lyn I married wouldn't have wanted me to do that—just as I wouldn't have wanted her to be on her own if I'd been the one who was killed and she was the one left behind,' he said. 'But it went sour for us because she wanted a family so desperately. And that's what's stopped me moving on. I don't want to go through that again, to lose the woman I love a little more each day and know I can't do anything to help.'

'I can understand that,' Grace said.

'But then I realised something,' he said. 'These last few days I've been running away again, burying myself in work so I didn't have to think or face things—but I'm ready to face them now.'

'Face what?' she asked.

'The fact that…' He took a deep breath. 'I love you, Grace. And I want to be with you. And I should've told you that as soon as we got back from Venice, instead of letting you come back here on your own.'

'I don't get it,' she said.

'You don't believe I love you?'

'I don't get why you're saying this to me now.

Nothing's changed since we came back from Venice.'

'Oh, but it has,' he corrected. 'I've had time to think. Time to miss you. And what finally made me realise was when I found the paperweight—and you thanked me for sweeping you off your feet.'

So did that mean…? The hope she'd ruthlessly squashed earlier flickered back into life.

'And I think you swept me off my feet, too,' he said. 'In just over two weeks, you taught me to have fun again. You taught me how to reconnect.'

'But I didn't really do anything,' she said. 'You're the one who did all the big romantic stuff and took me to places I'd always wanted to see. I don't even know what your dreams are, so I couldn't even begin to start making any of them come true.'

'I didn't know what my dreams were, either, but I do now,' he said. 'I want to live, really live, with the woman I love. A woman who's brave and funny and sweet.'

He couldn't possibly be describing her. 'But I'm not brave. Or funny. I'm just *ordinary*.'

'You're quiet and sensible and grounded,' he said, 'which is all good. But there's more to you than that. There's also a part of you that shines. The woman I danced with on the bank of the Seine, and who was brave enough to order lunch in Paris in schoolgirl French. The woman who likes to plan everything but who put herself out of her comfort zone for a few weeks. The woman who makes my world so much brighter just by being there. And I want you in my life for good, Grace. As my wife.'

But he'd been there before and it had all gone wrong. She couldn't just sweep that under the carpet. 'What about children?' she asked.

'Yet more proof that you're brave,' he said wryly, 'since you're not scared of dealing with a subject that would make most people shy away. Especially because you're the only other person in the world who knows the whole truth about Lyn and me.' He looked at her. 'I admit, part of me is scared to death about it. I've had one marriage go sour on me—and it's something I can't really talk about, because Lyn can't speak up for herself now and I don't want people to think badly of her.'

'Absolutely,' she agreed. 'And, just so you know, I don't think badly of her either.'

'Thank you.' He took a deep breath. 'I'm not confusing you with Lyn. I'm not seeing you as her replacement—I'm seeing you as you. But, even though I want to be with you, it scares me that I might end up repeating the same pattern.'

'How?' she asked.

'I don't want to see you get hurt and bogged down,' he said. 'When I asked you in the museum if you wanted children, you said there were no guarantees.'

'Because there aren't,' she said.

'I don't know if the problem was with Lyn or with me,' he said. 'If it was with me, then you and I might not be able to conceive. I hate the idea of going through all that again, knowing month after month that I've let you down. But,' he said, 'if having children is really important to you, I'll take that risk. I just need to know that...' He stopped. 'I'm making a mess of this.'

'You need to know that our relationship is about

more than just having children,' Grace said. 'I get it.' She paused. 'Do you want children, Roland?'

He nodded. 'But not at the cost of my marriage. I love you, Grace, and I want to marry you. But wanting everything is greedy.'

'You taught me something,' she said. 'You taught me that it's OK not to settle for things, not to stick rigidly to my fall-back position of being sensible. It's OK to dream. But you need to balance it with real life and you need to keep it in perspective. If having children naturally doesn't work for us, we can look at other options. Being a biological parent is no guarantee of being a good one. Ed isn't related to me by blood, but he's the best dad I could ever have asked for.'

'I agree with you. OK. So what happened to me and Lyn—that won't happen to us,' he said.

'Definitely not,' she confirmed. 'We won't let it.'

'You know when we touched that heart-shaped brick in Venice?'

She nodded.

'What did you wish for?'

'You asked me that before—and if you tell a wish it doesn't come true,' she reminded him.

'Actually, I got the legend wrong. Apparently, the real one is that if you touch the brick, you fall in love. If you touch the brick at the same time as someone else, you'll be devoted to each other for the rest of your days.' He paused. 'We touched the brick at the same time, Grace. I remember that very clearly.'

She felt the colour heating her cheeks. 'Yes.'

'And I fell in love with you. I think I fell in love with you before then, but that was when it hit me.' He raised an eyebrow. 'Do you want to know what I wished?'

'What did you wish?' Her words were a whisper.

'I wished that our arrangement was more than that. That it could be real. And carry on for the rest of our lives.'

Exactly the same as her own wish.

'So will you marry me, Grace?' he asked. 'Will you make my dreams come true?'

Every nerve in her body was urging her to say yes. To go for her dream. But her common sense still held her back. 'We've known each other only a few weeks, and you really think we can make a go of it?' She shook her head. 'But I'd known Howard for eighteen months before he proposed—six months as a colleague and a year as my boyfriend.'

'So you don't want to marry me?' His face went inscrutable.

'My heart's telling me to rush in and say yes,' she admitted, 'but I'm still scared. Like you, I've been there before and it's gone wrong. I was engaged to Howard for four years, Roland.'

'And you still hadn't bought your wedding dress, three weeks before the big day—when I know you're the super-organised type who likes planning things in advance,' he pointed out. 'So maybe you knew deep down that marriage wasn't the right thing for you and Howard, and you let it go as slowly as you could.'

'Maybe.'

Again, he lifted her hand to his mouth and kissed the backs of her fingers. 'His parents didn't like you, and they made you feel as if you were a worthless gold-digger. So I'm guessing that you're worried my family will feel that same way about you, too.'

She swallowed hard. 'Yes.'

'My family isn't like Howard's,' he said. 'They're not judgemental. They're eccentric and they have bossy tendencies—well, you've met Philly so you already know that bit for yourself— but they're warm and they'll love you to bits as soon as they meet you. And I definitely like everyone I've met in your family.'

'Uh-huh.' She bit her lip. 'Roland, I'm not very good about being spontaneous. And I know you're good at sweeping me off my feet, but that wouldn't be right—not for this. Can I have some time to think about it? Time to sort my head out?'

'Yes,' he said, 'but I'm not giving you time to worry about things. Come and meet my family tomorrow, so you can see for yourself that it'll be fine.'

She looked at him, horrified. 'That's not giving them much notice.'

He smiled. 'Are you telling me you wouldn't ring Bella or your parents on the spur of the moment and ask if you could drop in for a cup of tea? Or that they wouldn't drop in on you unexpectedly?'

'They're my family. That's what families do.'

'Exactly. And it's the same for me. So you'll come and meet them tomorrow?'

She didn't have any arguments left. And she knew she was right: the only way to get over her fears was to meet them. 'OK.'

'Good.'

'But I need you to know that I'll never come between you and your family. If they don't like me, then I'll fade out of your life,' she warned.

'Deal,' he said. 'And I need you to know that I'm absolutely certain that won't happen. They'll love you, Grace. They'll see you for who you are and they'll love you.' He kissed her lingeringly. 'More to the point, *I* love you.'

'I love you, too,' she said shyly.

'But you're worried that the past is going to repeat itself and you need to be sure it won't. I get that.' He smiled. 'And I'll wait until you're ready to give me an answer.'

CHAPTER ELEVEN

THE NEXT MORNING, Grace woke in Roland's arms. She lay there for a moment, just enjoying being close to him; but gradually she grew antsy.

Today was the day she was going to meet his family.

He'd said it would be light and easy. Just coffee. And he was sure they'd love her.

But what if they didn't? Howard's parents had never thought she was good enough for their son. And Roland's background was very different from her own.

She knew that if she lay there, she'd get more and more miserable, and she'd start fidgeting. She needed to be active; but she also didn't want to wake Roland and start whining at him.

When life gives you lemons, she thought, you make lemon drizzle cake.

And maybe that would be a good way to break the ice with Roland's family. She could take them some home-made lemon drizzle cake to go with the coffee.

Gently, she extracted herself from Roland's arms, shrugged on her dressing gown, crept out of the bedroom and quietly closed the door.

She'd just finished putting the hot lemon and sugar solution on the cake, letting it sink in, when Roland walked out of the bedroom.

'Sorry—did I wake you with all the noise?' she asked.

'No. But something smells amazing.'

'I thought I could take some cake with us,' she said.

He wrapped his arms round her and kissed the top of her head. 'Stop worrying. It'll be fine. But cake is good. You didn't make any spare, by any chance?'

'You'd eat cake for breakfast?'

'French family rules,' he said.

She laughed. 'Made-up rules, more like.'

'Busted.' He held her close. 'Grace, it's going to be fine. I promise.'

He took her mind off things by having a shower with her.

But her nerves returned, doubled, when he drove them to his family home and she could see the enormous house at the end of the long drive.

'Roland—this is a stately home!'

'It's not open to the public. Well, the gardens will be and we're going to do teas and weddings, but...' He shrugged. 'It's not a big deal.'

Yes, it was. She bit her lip. 'Roland, I come from a very ordinary background—and I'm not like Bel. I'm not all bubbly and bouncy and easy to love.'

'Your background is absolutely not an issue— and you're not ordinary, you're the woman I love,' he said firmly. 'Yes, I know you're a bit shy and it takes time to get to know you—but you're more than worth getting to know, and my family's perceptive. They'll see that straight away.'

Grace, remembering Cynthia Sutton's judgemental sneer and her habit of muttering disapproving comments behind the swing of her perfect bob, wasn't so sure. By the time Roland opened the front door, she was feeling physically sick.

But then two dogs came romping down the hallway, barking madly, with their tails wagging nineteen to the dozen.

'Morning, beasties. Coco's the poodle, after Chanel, and Napoleon's the basset hound,' Roland explained. 'French dogs, French names, yada-yada-yada.'

Grace made a fuss of the dogs, who insisted on licking every bit of her they could reach.

'Paws off the cake, beasties,' Roland said with a grin. 'Most of that is mine.'

And then the hall was full of people. Roland introduced them swiftly.

'Grace, these are my parents, Henry and Joanna; my brother Will and sister-in-law Susie; my sister Philly you've already met; and this is my niece, Matilda.'

'Hello,' Grace said shyly, holding out a hand.

But, to her shock, instead of shaking her hand, they all hugged her in turn; and that included little Matilda.

This was so very different from Howard's family; and so much more like her own.

'Coffee's ready,' Joanna said. 'Would you prefer to sit in the drawing room or the kitchen, Grace?'

Grace looked to Roland for an answer, but his face was impassive.

'The kitchen, please,' she said. 'And, um, I made you some cake. I hope that's OK.' She handed the plastic box to Joanna.

'Told you she was a keeper,' Philly said in a stage whisper.

'Shut up, Philly,' Roland said, in the same stage whisper. 'Sorry, Grace. But you've already met my sister. You know she's bossy.'

'Runs in the family,' Philly retorted, and put her arm round Grace. 'What kind of cake is it?'

'Lemon drizzle.'

'Yes! That makes you my new best friend,' Philly said with a grin.

'Actually,' Joanna said, 'I think the men should go and sit in the drawing room while we go and sort out cake and coffee in the kitchen.'

'Good idea,' Susie said with a smile.

'Hang on,' Roland began, his eyes widening. 'No interrog...'

But it was too late. Joanna swept Grace off to the kitchen along with Philly, Susie and Matilda. When Roland came in to try and rescue her, his mother just waved him away and said, 'This is a girls-only chat. Off you go, and close the door behind you.'

Roland gave Grace a helpless look, mouthed 'sorry', and did as he was told.

'We really are glad to meet you, Grace,' Joanna said, putting the cake on a plate. 'And this smells gorgeous. Did you make it this morning?'

'Yes. I, um—when I'm nervous, I bake,' Grace admitted.

'And meeting all of us for the first time is pretty scary,' Susie said. 'I remember what it feels like.'

'Though it's not all of us for the first time. You already know me,' Philly pointed out.

'And we feel we know you,' Joanna said, 'because Philly's told us about you.'

'There isn't actually that much to say about me,' Grace said. 'I'm very ordinary.'

'Tell us about you in your own words,' Susie invited.

This felt like a job interview, but she also knew that it was the most important interview she'd ever have in her life. If Roland's family couldn't accept her, then she'd fade out of his life—for his sake. 'I'm an accountant, I have a clean driving licence and I like cooking,' Grace said. 'I think that covers it.'

'I think there's something quite important you forgot to say,' Joanna said quietly. 'You've put the smile back into Roland's eyes. And to do that takes someone very out of the ordinary.'

'Seconded,' Philly said promptly.

'Thirded,' Susie added.

'Fourthed,' Matilda said, beaming at her. 'Can you make cupcakes, Grace? They're my favourite.'

'Chocolate or vanilla?' Grace asked.

Matilda thought about it. 'Both.'

Grace laughed. 'Good choice. Yes.'

'Are you going to marry Uncle Roland?'

Susie swept her daughter up and plonked her

on her lap. 'We're not supposed to ask that, sweet-pea.'

'Why not? I like Grace. So does Coco. I think she should marry Uncle Roland and then I can be the flower girl at the wedding,' Matilda said.

Susie groaned. 'I'm so sorry, Grace. She's obsessed with being a flower girl.'

'My best friend's been a flower girl three times already,' Matilda confided, 'and she's got a tiara with sparkly butterflies on it.'

'That sounds lovely,' Grace said, smiling.

'I think you should go and tell Daddy the cake's coming soon, Tilda,' Susie said, and Matilda slid off her lap and scampered out of the kitchen. 'I really am sorry about that,' she said to Grace.

'It's fine. Really,' Grace said.

'Out of the mouths of babes,' Philly said with a grin.

Then it hit Grace. This wasn't anything like her first meeting with the Suttons. Roland was right. She hadn't been judged and found wanting. His family was eccentric and bossy—and utterly lovely. And it felt as if they'd already taken her to their hearts.

'This,' she said, 'feels exactly like my parents' kitchen would if I had a brother who'd brought a girlfriend home to meet them for the first time.'

'Is that a good thing?' Joanna asked carefully.

Grace nodded. 'Because, although I don't have a brother, I do have a mother and a sister I love very much. And the best stepfather in the world.'

'That sounds good to me.' Joanna lifted her mug of coffee in a toast. 'We really are pleased to meet you, Grace. And I'm sorry for the interrogation.'

'No, we're not,' Philly admitted, not looking in the slightest bit abashed.

'Of course you're not,' Grace said, laughing back. 'Just as I wouldn't be in your shoes.'

'If it's any consolation, they did it to me, too,' Susie said, giving her a hug. 'And they're all right, this Devereux lot.'

The ice was well and truly broken then—especially when they re-joined the others in the drawing room and everyone tasted Grace's cake. 'You're officially in charge of cake from now on,' Will said. 'And we are so going to pick your brains for tea room suggestions.'

'Yes—Roland ought to show you the boathouse after lunch and tell you what he's planned,' Henry added. 'He can explain them better than any of us can.'

'Actually, I have new plans,' Roland said. 'I know exactly how we can make ourselves stand out for the wedding business.'

Grace had a feeling she knew what was coming next, and hid a smile.

'We could,' he suggested, 'build a folly. A mini-Pantheon.'

Merciless teasing followed.

'This lot has no vision,' he sighed theatrically. 'Grace, tell them you think it's a great idea.'

'I think I'll stick with what you said originally,' she said. 'In two hundred years' time, visitors to the house will be told that you were Roland the Mad Architect.'

'She's got your number, little brother,' Will said with a grin.

After lunch—and after Grace had absolutely insisted on being allowed to help with the washing up—Roland took Grace out to the boathouse and explained what they were planning to do.

'It's got the perfect outlook,' she said. 'And you're right. That wall of glass will give a spectacular view of the lake.'

On the way back to the house, he took her on a detour into the rose garden.

'Oh, now this is pretty,' she said in delight. 'And I've never smelled anything so lovely.'

'You'd need Philly to talk you through all the names and their history,' he said. 'But.' He paused by the sundial. 'You've met my family now.'

'Yes.'

'Do you like them?'

She smiled. 'They're lovely. And they remind me a lot of my family.'

'Good.' He paused. 'I know I said I'd give you time to think—but I really hate waiting. I'm sure that my life with you will be good. And, now you've met my family, I hope all your fears are set to rest, too.'

'They are,' she said.

He took something from his pocket and dropped to one knee. 'Grace. I love you. Will you marry me?' He opened the box and held it out to her.

Set on a bed of purple velvet was the prettiest

ring she'd ever seen: a solitaire diamond set in a star-shaped mount.

'A star,' he said, 'because you're *ma belle étoile*. And I really, really love you.'

Grace swallowed hard.

She'd asked him for time. But she didn't need it any more. 'I love you, too. Yes,' she whispered.

He slid the engagement ring onto her finger, then stood up, picked her up, whirled her round, and then kissed her until she was dizzy.

'I hope you're prepared for what happens next, because my family have a really bad habit of taking over,' he said.

'I'm with you, so I can be brave.' She smiled. 'Bring it on.'

It took Matilda all of five seconds to spot the difference when they walked in. 'Your hand—it's all sparkly!' she said in delight. 'Oh—it's a ring. And it's like a star!'

And Roland slid his arm round Grace's shoulders, clearly enjoying the spectacle of seeing his closest family stunned into silence. 'This has to be a first,' he said, laughing.

Everything suddenly went high-octane, with everyone talking at once.

'So when's the wedding? And it has to be here—every Devereux gets married here,' Will said.

'I have a friend who makes amazing dresses,' Susie said.

'*Croquembouche.* We need a proper *croquembouche* wedding cake,' Henry said. 'With sparklers. Lots of sparklers.'

'The flowers are mine, all mine,' Philly said, rubbing her hands together. 'I can't wait to make you the most beautiful bridal bouquet in the world.'

'And I can be the flower girl and have a sparkly tiara with butterflies!' Matilda crowed happily.

'Wait,' Joanna said, walking into the middle of the room and holding her hands up for silence, for all the world like a headmistress in the middle of a noisy assembly hall.

Grace felt her stomach drop. Had she made the wrong decision? Would Joanna feel the same way that Cynthia had—that Grace wasn't good enough for her son?

'Listen, you lot. I know this is the best news ever, but we have to remember that it's Grace and Roland's day,' Joanna said quietly. *'They're* the ones who make the decisions, not us. And we are absolutely not talking wedding plans without Grace's family being part of those discussions.'

So very unlike the way the Suttons had seen things, Grace thought with relief.

'OK. We'll have a planning meeting tomorrow—or as soon as Grace's family can get here,' Will said.

Roland coughed. 'Did you not hear what Mum said? And I agree. It's Grace's choice.'

Everyone stopped and looked at her.

They all wanted to be involved in her wedding, Grace realised. Not because they wanted to take over, the way that Howard's family had, but because they wanted to be part of it and make her and Roland's day truly special.

She knew without a doubt that, unlike Cynthia, they'd be more than happy for Bella to be her bridesmaid. Just as Grace would be very happy to ask Philly and Susie to be her bridesmaids and Matilda to be the flower girl—complete with her sparkly butterfly tiara. And butterfly wings, if she wanted them.

'My parents are in Italy right now,' she said, 'but they're due home next weekend. A planning meeting sounds good to me. And your house is beautiful. I can't think of anywhere nicer to get married.'

'In our private church,' Will said. 'Or in the house—I'm doing the paperwork to get licensed to hold weddings right now, and I'm sure I can rush it through if you need me to.'

'Or I could build the mini-Pantheon in the grounds,' Roland suggested. 'That'd be a really spectacular wedding venue.'

Everyone groaned. 'Roland. *No!*'

'Spoilsports,' Roland grumbled. But he was laughing.

'And, whatever anyone suggests, Grace gets the casting vote,' Henry added.

Coco and Napoleon barked, as if agreeing.

They were all on her side.

And Grace knew that this time everything was going to be just fine.

EPILOGUE

Three months later

ON A PERFECT Saturday afternoon in September, Grace got out of the car at the gates leading to Roland's ancestral home, and let her stepfather help her up into the old-fashioned coach pulled by four perfect white horses.

'You look beautiful, Gracie,' Ed said. 'Like a princess.'

'Thank you,' she said shyly.

'I know I'm not your real dad, but I'm so proud of you.'

She squeezed his hand. 'You're not my *biological* dad,' she corrected, 'but as far as I'm concerned you're my real dad and you have been ever since you came into my life. I'm a Faraday girl through and through. And you're the only person I would ever consider asking to walk me down the aisle.'

Moisture glittered in his eyes. 'Oh, Gracie.'

'Don't cry, Dad,' she warned, 'or I'll cry too, and Bella took ages doing my make-up—she'll kill us both if it smudges.'

'I love you,' he said, 'and I'm so glad you're marrying someone who loves you and will always back you.'

This was so very different from what she'd planned before. And even making the plans had been different this time, too: because both families had arranged things together.

The horses pulled the coach up the long driveway. Grace's mother, the bridesmaids and the photographer were waiting outside the little private church where every member of Roland's family had been married for the last three hundred years.

The photographer took shots of her in the coach with Ed; then Ed helped her out and her mother made last minute adjustments to her veil and dress.

'You look wonderful,' she said. 'Now go and

marry the love of your life, with all our love and blessings.'

Grace's smile felt a mile wide as she entered the church.

The string quartet—Hugh's latest signing—struck up the first movement of Karl Jenkins's *Palladio* as Grace walked down the aisle on Ed's arm. The chapel was filled with old-fashioned roses chosen by Philly from the formal gardens at the house, and the arrangements were echoed in the simple but elegant bouquets carried by Grace and her bridesmaids. Matilda walked in front of them, wearing her sparkly butterfly tiara and scattering rose petals. Grace could see Roland waiting for her at the aisle, and saw his brother Will nudge him and whisper something just before he looked round.

As he saw her walking down the aisle towards him, he smiled and mouthed, 'I love you,' and the whole world felt as if it had just lit up.

She couldn't stop smiling through the whole service. Finally, the vicar said, 'You may now kiss the bride.' And Roland did so lingeringly.

There were more photographs outside the

church and in the rose garden; then they finally walked down to the lake, where the boathouse was newly renovated and ready to host its first ever wedding breakfast. The wall overlooking the lake was completely glass, giving perfect views across the lake; and as they looked out they could see swans gliding across the water.

'This is so perfect,' Grace whispered.

Roland kissed her. 'It certainly is.'

The tables were set with more beautiful arrangements of roses and the last of the sweet peas. 'Like the first flowers you ever bought me,' she said to Roland with a smile. 'Philly's really done us proud.'

Everything was perfect, from the meal to the speeches and the music from Hugh's quartet. And Grace knew that it was going to get even better; they had a band for the evening reception, and Roland had planned a display of fireworks just behind the lake.

And there were fireworks indoors, too: because to Henry's pleasure they'd gone with his suggestion of using a tradition from the French side of the family, and instead of a tiered wedding cake they had a *croquembouche* with a spiral of white chocolate roses curled round it. At the top of the cone, instead of a sugar crown there was an array of indoor sparklers; as soon as they were lit, everyone oohed and aahed.

'It's magical,' Grace said.

'Absolutely. And that's how it's going to be for the rest of our life,' Roland agreed. 'With our whole family behind us, helping us to make our dreams come true.'

She raised her glass of sparkling elderflower cordial to toast him. 'For the rest of our life.' She paused. 'Roland, do you think we can sneak out for a moment without anyone noticing?'

'Why?'

'Because...' She needed to tell him something, but she wanted to tell him in private, and so far she just hadn't found the right moment. 'I need a moment with you. Alone.'

'And you want us to sneak out, given that all eyes are on the bride and groom?' He grinned. 'Well, hey. We're a team. We can do anything.' He put her glass down on a nearby table, and waltzed with her over to the corner of the room, then quietly danced with her until they were at a side door. 'Righty. Let's slip out.'

Once they were outside, he found them a quiet spot by the lake. 'OK. From the look on your face, it's not just because you want to be on your own with your new husband. What's wrong?'

'Nothing's wrong. But… What you were saying about us being a team. A team means more than two, or it can mean a pair.'

'You're splitting hairs, but OK,' he said. 'You and me. Two. We're a pair, then.'

She coughed. 'I'm trying to tell you something. We're a *team*.'

'You just said we were a pair.'

'But,' she said, 'we went to Venice just over three months ago. We made love for the first time.'

'Ye—es.' He frowned. 'You're talking in riddles, Gracie.'

'No, I'm not.' She stroked his face. 'I thought architects were good with figures? And have an eye for detail?'

'We do.'

'So did you notice that I toasted you in elderflower cordial, not champagne?' she asked. 'And alcohol is off the menu for me for the next six months. Along with soft cheese and lightly cooked eggs.'

She saw the second that the penny dropped. 'Are you telling me...?' he asked, hope brightening his face.

'I know we didn't plan it, but we're definitely Team Devereux,' she said. 'I didn't want to tell you until I was completely sure—and I wanted you to be the very first to know. I thought I might be a bit late just because I've been rushing about sorting out wedding stuff. Not because I was stressed, because our joint family is brilliant, but just because...it's a wedding.' She spread her hands. 'And it's not that. Because I did a test this morning.'

'And it was positive?'

'It was positive,' she confirmed.

'I don't care that we didn't plan having a baby. It's the best wedding present ever,' he said, picking her up and whirling her round. 'I love you—both of you.' He set her back down on the ground and cupped his hand protectively over her abdomen. 'Team Devereux. You, me, and a baby that's going to have the best family in the world.'

'The best family in the world,' she echoed.

* * * * *

MILLS & BOON®
Large Print – August 2016

The Sicilian's Stolen Son
Lynne Graham

Seduced into Her Boss's Service
Cathy Williams

The Billionaire's Defiant Acquisition
Sharon Kendrick

One Night to Wedding Vows
Kim Lawrence

Engaged to Her Ravensdale Enemy
Melanie Milburne

A Diamond Deal with the Greek
Maya Blake

Inherited by Ferranti
Kate Hewitt

The Billionaire's Baby Swap
Rebecca Winters

The Wedding Planner's Big Day
Cara Colter

Holiday with the Best Man
Kate Hardy

Tempted by Her Tycoon Boss
Jennie Adams

0716 Rom LP

MILLS & BOON®
Large Print – September 2016

Morelli's Mistress
Anne Mather

A Tycoon to Be Reckoned With
Julia James

Billionaire Without a Past
Carol Marinelli

The Shock Cassano Baby
Andie Brock

The Most Scandalous Ravensdale
Melanie Milburne

The Sheikh's Last Mistress
Rachael Thomas

Claiming the Royal Innocent
Jennifer Hayward

The Billionaire Who Saw Her Beauty
Rebecca Winters

In the Boss's Castle
Jessica Gilmore

One Week with the French Tycoon
Christy McKellen

Rafael's Contract Bride
Nina Milne

MILLS & BOON®

Why shop at millsandboon.co.uk?

Each year, thousands of romance readers find their perfect read at millsandboon.co.uk. That's because we're passionate about bringing you the very best romantic fiction. Here are some of the advantages of shopping at www.millsandboon.co.uk:

* **Get new books first**—you'll be able to buy your favourite books one month before they hit the shops

* **Get exclusive discounts**—you'll also be able to buy our specially created monthly collections, with up to 50% off the RRP

* **Find your favourite authors**—latest news, interviews and new releases for all your favourite authors and series on our website, plus ideas for what to try next

* **Join in**—once you've bought your favourite books, don't forget to register with us to rate, review and join in the discussions

Visit **www.millsandboon.co.uk**
for all this and more today!